ABOUT THE AUTHOR

Barbara Cartland, the world's most famous romantic novel-
ist, who is also an historian, playwright, lecturer, political
speaker and television personality, has now written over 530
books and sold over 500 million copies all over the world.

She has also had many historical works published and has
written four autobiographies as well as the biographies of her
mother and that of her brother, Ronald Cartland, who was
the first Member of Parliament to be killed in the last war.
This book has a preface by Sir Winston Churchill and has just
been republished with an introduction by the late Sir Arthur
Bryant.

"Love at the Helm" a novel written with the help and
inspiration of the late Earl Mountbatten of Burma, Great
Uncle of His Royal Highness The Prince of Wales, is being
sold for the Mountbatten Memorial Trust.

She has broken the world record for the last sixteen years
by writing an average of twenty-three books a year. In the
Guinness Book of Records she is listed as the world's
top-selling author.

Miss Cartland in 1978 sang an Album of Love Songs with
the Royal Philharmonic orchestra.

In private life Barbara Cartland, who is a Dame of Grace of
the Order of St. John of Jerusalem, Chairman of the St. John
Council in Hertfordshire and Deputy President of the St.
John Ambulance Brigade, has fought for better conditions
and salaries for Midwives and Nurses.

She championed the cause for the Elderly in 1956 invoking
a Government Enquiry into the "Housing Conditions of Old
People".

In 1962 she had the Law of England changed so that Local
Authorities had to provide camps for their own Gypsies. This
has meant that since then thousands and thousands of Gypsy
children have been able to go to School which they had never
been able to do in the past, as their caravans were moved
every twenty-four hours by the Police.

There are now fourteen camps in Hertfordshire and Barbara Cartland has her own Romany Gypsy Camp called
Barbaraville by the Gypsies.

Her designs "Decorating with Love" are being sold all over
the U.S.A. and the National Home Fashions League made

her in 1981, "Woman of Achievement".

Barbara Cartland's book "Getting Older, Growing Younger" has been published in Great Britain and the U.S.A. and her fifth Cookery Book, "The Romance of Food" is now being used by the House of Commons.

In 1984 she received at Kennedy Airport, America's Bishop Wright Air Industry Award for her contribution to the development of aviation. In 1931 she and two R.A.F. Officers thought of, and carried the first aeroplane-towed glider air-mail.

During the War she was Chief Lady Welfare Officer in Bedfordshire looking after 20,000 Service men and women. She thought of having a pool of Wedding Dresses at the War Office so a Service Bride could hire a gown for the day.

She bought 1,000 secondhand gowns without coupons for the A.T.S., the W.A.A.F.s and the W.R.E.N.S. In 1945 Barbara Cartland received the Certificate of Merit from Eastern Command.

In 1964 Barbara Cartland founded the National Association for Health of which she is the President, as a front for all the Health Stores and for any product made as alternative medicine.

This has now a £650,000,000 turnover a year, with one third going in export.

In January 1988 she received "La Medaille de Vermeil de la Ville de Paris", (the Gold Medal of Paris). This is the highest award to be given by the City of Paris for ACHIEVE-MENT – 25 million books sold in France.

In March 1988 Barbara Cartland was asked by the Indian Government to open their Health Resort outside Delhi. This is almost the largest Health Resort in the world.

Barbara Cartland was made a Dame of the Order of the British Empire in the 1991 New Year's Honours List.

The Scent of Roses

The Marquis of Ridgmont, who has been having an *affaire de coeur* with Lady Lessington, escapes retribution and a national scandal by accepting the Prime Minister Lord Beaconsfield's proposal that he goes on a secret mission to see what is happening in the war between Russia and Turkey.

He is about to set off when he discovers that Sir James Tancombe, an ardent collector of pictures who is obsessed by his Ancient Family House, has been stealing.

To save another scandal of a different sort, he punishes Sir James by sending him off to Peru to look at the 17th Century pictures which were being neglected in Cuzco.

To make his visit to Constantinople seem just a holiday trip, he insists that Sir James' sister, the beautiful innocent Nikola goes with him as a companion.

How Nikola is very different from what the Marquis expected, how she saves his life and how they eventually find happiness, is told in this romantic 428th book by Barbara Cartland.

BARBARA CARTLAND

The Scent of Roses

Mandarin

THE SCENT OF ROSES

First published in Great Britain 1991
by Mandarin Paperbacks
Michelin House, 81 Fulham Road, London SW3 6RB

Mandarin is an imprint of the Octopus Publishing Group,
a division of Reed International Books Limited.

Copyright © Cartland Promotions 1991

A CIP catalogue record for this title
is available from the British Library
ISBN 0 7493 0833 8 PB
ISBN 0 7493 0994 X HB

Printed in Great Britain
by St Edmundsbury Press Ltd, Bury St Edmunds, Suffolk

AUTHOR'S NOTE

Tsar Alexander II disliked war, but the Empress wanted to reinstate Constantinople as the greatest City in Christendom.

The Russians had an age-old dream of opening the Straits to Russian Ships.

In 1875, Serbia declared war on Turkey and thousands of Russian Volunteers poured into Belgrade.

After the uprising in Bulgaria, the terrible reprisals of the Turks were described by a British Diplomat as:

"The most horrendous crime of the Century!"

In Britain the Leader of the Opposition, Mr. Gladstone, took up the cause fiercely and the people applauded him.

The Prime Minister, Lord Beaconsfield was, however, conscious that the only country that the Russians feared on their march on Constantinople was Britain.

The Tsar, pressured by his brother The Grand Duke Nicholas as well as the Empress, finally declared war in the Spring of 1877, which is where this story begins.

What the Marquis suggested as a show of strength actually took place.

The conflict lasted nine months and due to Britain's intervention the Russians never took Constantinople and were denied access to the Mediterranean which they had hoped to reach through Bulgaria.

As Lord Beaconsfield said gleefully to Queen Victoria:

"Prince Gorchakov says: 'We have sacrificed one hundred-thousand picked soldiers and one hundred million pounds for nothing!' "

When I visited Cuzco in 1977, there were still many beautiful 17th Century paintings fading in the sun, bulging out of their frames and being allowed to rot through neglect.

The Virgin in the Rose Garden by Lochner is now in the Louvre in Paris.

CHAPTER ONE
1877

Nikola walked across the garden.

She was thinking as she did so how beautiful the house was.

"King's Keep" had been in her family since the reign of Henry VIII.

It had been used as a Hunting Lodge for Queen Elizabeth.

It was, Nikola thought, redolent not only with history but also with the ghosts of the past.

She could understand why her brother loved it more than anything else in the world.

Laughingly she often said to him:

"Any wife, if you ever had one, will be desperately jealous of King's Keep."

"It is mine!" he said fiercely. "Mine, and no one shall take it from me!"

He had talked like that ever since he was a small boy.

Yet now, as she thought about what he was doing so that King's Keep could continue being his, she shivered.

She was expecting him now.

She wondered apprehensively what he would have to tell her.

"How can we go on in this way?" she asked.

She was looking at the house as she spoke.

But it was really a prayer to her mother.

Nikola thought she would understand better than her father how dangerously her brother was behaving.

In a way she could understand.

It was agonising for him to see the house falling into disrepair.

He did not have enough money to keep it as perfect as it had been.

Sir James Tancombe was the 10th Baronet and exceedingly proud of his lineage.

Nikola often thought if King's Keep were taken away from him he would die of a broken heart.

They had very few servants.

She helped those there were almost from the moment she got up in the morning until she went to bed.

If there was a speck of dust, if a piece of furniture wanted polishing, or one of the beautiful old embroidered curtains needed mending, James's eagle eye would see it.

It hurt him as if it was a wound in his flesh.

This morning, because he was coming home, Nikola had inspected all the rooms.

She had made quite certain he would be unable to find anything wrong.

She could still remember the agony in his eyes when a year ago the ceiling fell in one of the bedrooms.

It was after that, they had almost starved themselves.

They had to find the money to repair it.

Then Jimmy, as she called her brother, had said:

"This cannot go on, and I know exactly what I am going to do!"

"What is that?" Nikola asked.

She was not hopeful that he would think of anything really helpful.

Only a week earlier one of their relatives had said harshly:

"It is no use, James, I cannot help you any more, and

the best thing you can do is to sell King's Keep. After all, it is only a house!"

Nikola had seen the fury in her brother's eyes.

She knew King's Keep was not just a house to him.

It was everything – everything that mattered.

Everything that was important, everything that gave him a sense of stability.

She could remember when he was young the happiness in his eyes when he returned home from School.

"I am home! I am home!" he would shout.

It was not really his father and mother he had missed. But King's Keep.

She hoped they would not know how shocked she had been when she had realised what he was doing.

He had taken her to stay with an ancient Aunt.

She had been a Tancombe before she married Lord Hartley.

Now she was a widow and very wealthy.

Nikola thought however, it was extremely unlikely that Jimmy would get a penny out of her.

Yet she was sure that was the purpose of their visit.

They had driven down the narrow, twisting lanes which made their journey a tiring one.

All the way there she was wishing they had stayed at home.

It was Jimmy who had suggested they should stay with their aunt.

Nikola knew he hoped to persuade her to give him enough money for repairs.

They were urgently needed on the roof.

Moreover some of the diamond panes of the windows needed replacing, and the floors in several of the main rooms were cracking.

They needed to be relaid with stronger supports.

She thought her brother was going to be disappointed.

11

His charm which fascinated most women, would be wasted on their Aunt Alice.

She had therefore said rather tentatively:

"You know, Jimmy dear, Aunt Alice is very mean, and Nanny told us the last time we stayed there that there was hardly enough to eat in the Servants' Hall."

"I know that," Jimmy replied.

"She never gives a penny to charity, and Nanny says she even begrudges the flowers she puts on her husband's grave."

Jimmy laughed.

"I thought I had heard all that before, but this is a new story!"

"Then do you really think," Nikola said, "that she will listen to you pleading for money to repair King's Keep?"

"I am not going to ask her for a penny!" her brother replied.

Nikola stared at him in astonishment.

"You are not?" she exclaimed. "Then why are we going to stay with her?"

"I will tell you later," Jimmy replied evasively.

They arrived at the large, rather ugly house.

It stood in a large garden with woods behind it.

The garden was not well kept.

Lady Hartley economised on the number of gardeners she employed.

As they went in through the front door, Nikola noticed that the Butler's coat was almost threadbare.

Even the footman's liveried waist-coat was almost in shreds.

"I cannot imagine," she said to herself, "why Jimmy insists on coming to this depressing place."

Her Aunt was waiting for them in the Drawing-Room.

"Oh, here you are!" she exclaimed when they appeared. "It is nice to see you. At the same time, it makes a lot of extra work for the staff."

12

"It is too long since we visited you," Jimmy said with one of his charming smiles, "and you know, Aunt Alice, I feel, as head of the family, I should keep in touch with all my relations."

"Personally I should have thought it a waste of time," Lady Hartley said sharply, "but now you are here I suppose you would like a glass of sherry?"

"It is certainly something I would welcome after the dust on the roads," Jimmy replied.

He was given a minute glass.

There was only enough sherry in it to be swallowed in two or three sips.

Nikola, being a young girl, was offered nothing.

She was very thirsty.

She was glad when she went up to change for dinner to drink the water that was in a glass bottle on the wash-stand.

There was not any water for her to drink at dinner.

It was a sparse meal, although the chicken lunch that was the main course came from the Home Farm.

Jimmy was allowed two glasses of a rather indifferent white wine.

He was also given a small glass of port.

He, however, talked charmingly to Lady Hartley, telling her stories of their other relatives.

He also paid her compliments which were obviously a novelty.

She accepted them with a certain amount of coyness.

When they moved into the Drawing-Room he said:

"I never realised before, Aunt Alice, what a vast number of pictures you have, and I am also very impressed by your collection of snuff-boxes."

"I did not collect them," Lady Hartley replied. "Your Uncle Edward wasted a great deal of money buying things that were of interest only to him."

"Well, they interest me!" Jimmy said. "So I am going to

take the opportunity, now I am here, to look at everything that Uncle Edward treasured, as I should do if they were mine."

"I should have thought you had enough 'Treasures', as you call them, at King's Keep!" Lady Hartley said tartly.

"One can never have too much of a good thing," Jimmy replied.

He got up as he spoke and started to walk round the Drawing-Room.

He looked at the pictures.

Then he inspected the collection of snuff-boxes which were in glass-topped cabinets.

He then left the room, explaining that he wanted to inspect some of the other rooms.

Lady Hartley started to tell Nikola of the difficulties of getting good servants.

The extravagance of the younger ones appalled her who preferred to throw away a torn sheet rather than darn it.

Jimmy was away for a long time.

Nikola could not imagine what there was to interest him in this ugly house.

The pictures might be good, but they needed cleaning.

The lack of light did not show them off to their best advantage.

The walls on which they hung were painted with drab colours.

Or else papered with what she thought were extremely dull designs.

When Jimmy returned to the Drawing-Room he congratulated his Aunt on the way the house was kept.

"I see, Aunt Alice," he said, "you expect perfection, as I do. But it is sad to see so many rooms shut up and apparently unused."

"I cannot afford to have a lot of people staying with me," Lady Hartley answered. "What do I want with a lot of chattering magpies, or to be asked to Balls and Receptions which are only for the 'Idle Rich'?"

Nikola gave her a wistful smile.

"I would love to attend a Ball," she said, "and perhaps next year, when we are out of mourning, Jimmy will be able to arrange it."

"If you are thinking of having a Season in London, it is something I am quite certain you cannot afford!" Lady Hartley said.

She did not see the disappointment in Nikola's eyes, but went on:

"A friend was telling me only a few days ago what it cost for her daughter to be a débutante and – would you believe it? – after all the trouble she went to, the stupid girl never received a single proposal of marriage!"

"I . . I suppose her parents . . had hoped that . . by taking her to London . . she would find a . . husband," Nikola said a little hesitatingly.

"Of course they did!" Lady Hartley agreed. "But it does not surprise me that the young women of today find it difficult to get one, seeing that their . . "

Nikola did not listen any more.

She had already heard her aunt's views about the young.

"They are uppish and impertinent!" she exclaimed.

There was no point in arguing.

Of one thing Nikola was quite certain: if she wished to shine in London Society, their Aunt would not assist her in any way.

She would, in fact, not offer to pay for so much as a petticoat, let alone a gown.

She wondered if that was one of the reasons why Jimmy had brought her here.

She could have told him, if he had asked her, that it was a waste of time.

They said good-bye the next morning.

It was obvious to Nikola that their aunt was pleased to see them go.

She thought Lady Hartley begrudged every mouthful they had consumed.

"I hope you will come to see us at King's Keep," Jimmy said politely as they said good-bye.

"It is too far for my horses," his Aunt replied.

As they drove down the drive Nikola said:

"I do hope we shall not have to go there again! The beds are uncomfortable, and mine was short of blankets." She looked at her brother as she spoke.

She saw to her surprise that he was smiling.

"You cannot really have enjoyed yourself, Jimmy?" she exclaimed. "I cannot imagine how Papa, who was always such fun and so very generous, could have such a stingy old sister as that!"

"Nor can I," Jimmy replied. "But do you realise that house is packed with Collectors' items?"

"Do you mean the pictures?" Nikola asked.

"Uncle Edward knew what he was doing when he bought them," Jimmy said, "and they must have gone up in value a dozen times since."

Nikola shrugged her shoulders.

"I cannot see how that helps us."

Jimmy did not reply.

When they arrived back at King's Keep he came into the Drawing-Room.

Nikola, who was repairing a piece of tapestry on one of the chairs, looked up.

She saw that Jimmy had changed his clothes.

He was carrying something in his hands.

"Have you unpacked?" she asked. "There was no reason to. I will do it after tea."

"I have unpacked," Jimmy replied, "because I have something to show you."

He put what he was carrying down on the table.

16

Nikola got up to walk towards him.

She saw that he was holding two very pretty miniatures and an oil-painting.

"What are those?" she asked.

"I found the picture in one of the upstairs rooms which are shut up and never used," Jimmy replied.

"Upstairs rooms?" Nikola repeated.

Then she gave a little cry.

"You mean . . they are Aunt Alice's? Oh, Jimmy, how could you have taken them away with you?"

"Very easily," he answered, "and I am certain that the old girl will never notice they are missing!"

Nikola gave a cry.

"But, Jimmy, – that is . . stealing!"

"In a good cause," he replied. "The money I will get for these will repair the roof!"

Nikola stared at him in horror.

"But . . you cannot mean . . to sell them? But, Jimmy, you could go to prison for theft!"

"That is a risk I shall have to take," Jimmy replied, "and what is the point of that old hag sitting on a 'gold mine'? She does not appreciate them, and certainly has no intention of sharing them with anybody else."

Nikola could only stare at him.

She thought how shocked her mother would be.

Jimmy was stealing, even if it was for his beloved house.

"And . . the . . miniatures?" she faltered after a moment.

"I found those in a drawer of Uncle Edward's desk in the Study. He must have bought them just before he died, and did not have time to hang them."

He touched one gently.

"They are both over two hundred years old, and there is no reason, if I sell them, why anybody should connect them with him."

"J.Just suppose . . somebody . . guessed they did not . . belong to you?"

"Who is likely to do that?" Jimmy asked. "As far as I can gather from the way Aunt Alice was speaking, she did not encourage any of the family to visit her."

He saw the stricken look in his sister's eyes.

He put his arms round her.

"Now be sensible, Nikola," he said. "We have to save King's Keep, and what I have done in taking these will not hurt anybody."

"But . . it is wrong . . I know it is . . wrong!" Nikola murmured.

"Then I suppose this will upset you," Jimmy said.

He put his hand in his pocket.

He drew out something very small which he placed in the palm of his hand.

It glittered in the sunshine coming through the window.

"What . . is it?" Nikola asked in a frightened voice.

"It is a diamond!"

"Where did you . . get it?"

"From one of the snuff-boxes."

Nikola made a stifled sound of horror but Jimmy went on:

"If, which is very unlikely, Aunt Alice or anyone else notices it has gone, they will just think it has fallen out, perhaps years ago."

Nikola did not speak.

After a moment Jimmy said:

"You will learn that people cease after a time to notice things that are familiar, things that have always been there."

That was true, Nikola was to find in the next few months.

Jimmy sold what he had taken for what seemed to her to be a large sum of money.

18

She thought he would be satisfied.

It certainly mended the roof and repaired the windows and the floors.

All the time there were workmen in the house Nikola tried to persuade herself that what Jimmy had done was not really wrong.

The money had been spent in preserving something of historic value.

At the same time, she prayed that he would not be punished.

Her mother would definitely have thought of it as a sin.

When the money had all been spent she realised Jimmy was restless.

"The curtains in the hall are faded," he said, "and something should be done about it."

"That is certainly something we cannot afford," Nikola said without thinking.

Then she saw the expression on her brother's face.

She felt as if a cold hand gripped her heart.

"Oh no Jimmy!" she cried. "You are not thinking . ."

But it was what he was thinking.

A week later he told her they were going to stay with another relative.

This one lived in an isolated part of Norfolk.

He was a Cousin who had married a woman very much richer than he was.

Her blood was not as "blue" as his.

The Tancombe family had always suspected that her money came from trade.

They had two rather plain daughters, both of marriagable age.

The moment they arrived Nikola was aware that they considered that Jimmy as the 10th Baronet, was a good matrimonial catch.

The house was certainly in contrast to the cheese-paring

and discomfort they had endured with Lady Hartley.

Colonel Arthur Tancombe and his wife lived in the most luxurious fashion.

There were four footmen in the hall and two housemaids to unpack Nikola's small trunk.

There was champagne to drink before dinner.

Different wines were served with every course.

Their cousins both had been presented at Court the previous year.

The Colonel and his wife had given them a Ball in London, and were planning another in the country.

It was only regrettable that they were both exceedingly plain.

They looked, Nikola discovered,their best on a horse.

Jimmy, however, put himself out to be charming.

Not only to the two girls, but also to Mrs. Tancombe.

They were delighted with him.

"Your brother is a delightful young man," she said to Nikola. "I cannot understand why he has not married."

"I am afraid it is something he cannot afford," Nikola replied.

"There are a great number of heiresses looking for a husband," Mrs. Tancombe said rather pointedly.

Later in the evening she confided to Nikola that Adelaide, her elder daughter, had accepted a proposal of marriage.

It was from a man who had nothing to offer her but his family tree.

"There were however, no titles in his family," Mrs. Tancombe explained, "and as he was thirty-nine, we felt he was really too old for Adelaide."

"Much too old," Nikola agreed. "And I do hope she finds somebody she loves."

Mrs. Tancombe laughed.

"My mother always said to me that love comes after

marriage, but I was very fortunate, and fell in love with my husband as soon as I saw him."

Looking at the Colonel Nikola thought he had undoubtedly been very handsome in his youth.

Good looks ran in the Tancombe family.

It was just unfortunate that his two daughters resembled their mother.

It was Mrs. Tancombe's money that had furnished the house in such an extravagant manner.

The pictures, however, had been collected by generations of the Colonel's family.

Nikola was not surprised that Jimmy was looking at them with interest.

"It is nice to think you care about such things," she heard the Colonel say to him. "I always wanted a son who would bear my name."

"I am particularly interested in the family portraits," Jimmy replied, "and I see you have quite a collection of early Masters."

"They belonged to my great-grandfather," the Colonel answered. "He bought this house, I have always believed, simply because it had plenty of wall space!"

He laughed.

"Well, he certainly covered it," Jimmy replied.

Escorted by the Colonel, he went from room to room.

In one he noticed there was a collection of small Chinese bowls.

"Where did these come from?" he asked.

"That was another relative, a distant Cousin," the Colonel explained. "He left the collection to my father when he died, but I cannot say I find it very attractive. I prefer the pictures."

"So do I," Jimmy agreed. When they returned to King's Keep he showed Nikola three Chinese bowls.

"This one is Ming, this is Sung, and the last is the Ch'ing dynasty," he told her.

"Are they very . . valuable?" she asked.

"They are unique – priceless!" Jimmy answered.

"And . . you have . . stolen them," Nikola murmured beneath her breath.

"Only from somebody who does not appreciate them! Therefore he has no right to anything so splendid!"

"But . . supposing the Colonel . . notices they have . . gone?"

"It is very unlikely," Jimmy replied. "He is only inter- ested in pictures, and I would be surprised if he has ever counted the bowls or anything else in the house."

There was no use telling Jimmy she thought it wrong.

He went to London the next day.

He came back wildly elated with what he had obtained for the bowls from a Connoisseur of Oriental pottery.

"He told me he had never dreamt of being lucky enough to find such perfect specimens," Jimmy boasted.

"He is . . not going to . . sell them again?" Nikola asked anxiously.

"No, fortunately. He wishes to keep them for himself."

Nikola gave a sigh of relief.

She had been afraid that if a lot of the bowls were put up for sale they might be written up in the newspapers.

Then the Colonel might think they were just the same as some he owned.

She lay awake all night worrying about the Chinese bowls.

But by the end of the year she had grown used to Jimmy taking her to stay with some remote relative.

Only once did they come away empty-handed.

That was because Jimmy had found nothing in the house that was really worth taking.

She had to admit that the improvements to King's Keep made the whole house glow like a precious jewel.

The ancient pink bricks were repointed.

The windows and the door were painted.

Then one by one, the rooms inside were redecorated.

It was beginning to look very lovely.

But Nikola held her breath every time a visitor admired it.

She was always afraid they would wonder how it had all been paid for.

Now as she reached the house she was aware that Jimmy should be back within the hour.

He had gone to London to sell a picture.

He had found it in the last house where they had stayed.

It belonged to a distant relative, Lord Mersey, who was a widower.

He had no children but was, Jimmy said, very close.

That meant, Nikola knew, he had refused at one time or another to lend him any money.

Lord Mersey had been born a Tancombe.

He had become a Peer when after a distinguished career at the Bar and on the Bench he had finally become a Lord of Appeal in Ordinary.

It was quite a large picture.

When he had carried it into her bedroom late at night she had exclaimed:

"But . . you cannot take . . that! It is so big that they will know at once that . . it has gone!"

"It is 17th century, and by Dughet. French artists who studied in Italy are beginning to fetch large prices," Jimmy said in a hard voice.

"W. Where did you . . find it?"

"In the big Servants' Hall which is only used when they have shooting parties."

"Surely the . . servants will see it has . . gone?" Nikola questioned.

Jimmy smiled.

"You under-rate me, my dear little sister! I have replaced it with a eleograph which I am certain they will admire far more than this!"

Nikola drew in her breath.

"It is . . the same . . size?"

"Almost exactly! I found that in a passage on the top floor where no one will miss it!"

As he spoke he wiped his handkerchief gently over the picture to remove the dust.

"This is going to give us the new curtains for the Dining-Room," he said, "and will pay the wages for another man in the garden."

There was a note in his voice which told Nikola it was no use arguing with him.

He was like a man in love.

He would do anything, however disreputable, for King's Keep.

He had brought the picture to Nikola's room because her trunk was already half-packed.

It was ready for them to leave the following morning.

"I have so few things with me," Jimmy said, "that the Valet would notice this picture if I carried it in my luggage."

"I do not want it in mine!" Nikola said quickly.

Even as she spoke she knew it was no use saying that to her brother.

He opened her trunk and lifted out the clothes which her maid had already packed and were neatly folded.

He placed the picture at the bottom.

He then put back the clothes he had taken out.

"Now you pack the rest," he said, "and make quite certain your maid does not rummage about if she puts in anything that has been left until the last minute."

Nikola found it impossible to sleep.

She was so frightened.

But they left without anybody suspecting that they carried away with them a picture.

Jimmy had taken it to London.

She told herself she should not be interested.

24

Yet she longed to hear what he had obtained for it.

As she entered the house she heard the sound of carriage-wheels outside the front-door.

She did not wait for Butters.

He was suffering from rheumatism and therefore was slow on his feet.

She pulled open the door.

Jimmy stepped out of the carriage in which he had been travelling.

She knew by the expression on his face that all was well.

"You are home! You are home! Oh, Jimmy, I am so glad to see you!" she cried.

He bent to kiss her cheek, then said:

"Yes, I am back, and I have some very exciting news to tell you!"

He walked into the house.

Butters, who had arrived belatedly from the kitchen-quarters, collected his luggage.

They entered the Drawing-Room which overlooked the garden.

"What has happened?" Nikola asked in a conspiratorial tone.

"A great deal," Jimmy replied. "I have obtained a thousand guineas for the picture!"

Nikola gave a gasp.

"As much as that?"

"More important," her brother went on, "we have been invited to stay with the Marquis of Ridgmont, and we are going there next Friday."

"The . . Marquis of . . R.Ridgmont?" Nikola repeated, thinking she had not heard of him before.

"His is one of the largest collections of pictures in the country," Jimmy said, "and it was he who bought the Dughet from me."

Nikola clasped her hands together.

"You are . . quite certain," she said in a voice little above a whisper, "that he did not suspect . . ?"

"No, no, of course not," Jimmy replied. "Why should he? As I told you, the picture was in the Servants' Hall."

Nikola gave a little shiver.

She thought it would be a mistake for Jimmy to become involved with Collectors.

They would know a great deal about pictures, and who owned them.

She had heard her father talk of various of his friends who were knowledgeable about antiques of every sort.

One was a collector of French furniture.

His ancestor had brought a great deal of it back from France after the Revolution.

There was another who had a passion for silver.

He attended every sale of it in London.

He also kept a record of the silver owned by great families.

She felt that as long as James concentrated on obtaining small pieces like the miniatures and even the Chinese bowls, he was more or less safe.

But moving amongst experts was surely a mistake

As if he knew what she was thinking, Jimmy said:

"Oh, do stop worrying! I can feel it vibrating from you."

"I . . I cannot . . help it," Nikola said. "You know, dearest, that if there was the . . slightest suspicion . . that you were a . . thief . . you would . . even if you did not go to . . prison . . be ostracised by everyone including our own . . f.family."

"It is easy to be honest and cautionary when you are rich," Jimmy remarked, "and as I have only stolen from people who do not appreciate what they own I do not feel in the least guilty!"

Nikola sighed.

She could understand her brother feeling like that and how much he wanted money for King's Keep.

He might try to justify what he was doing but it was still stealing.

She knew how unhappy it would have made her mother.

Her father would have been very angry.

"Now stop being like a wet rag and listen to what I have planned," Jimmy said sharply.

"I . . am listening," Nikola said in a very small voice.

"We are going to Huntingdonshire to stay in one of the finest and most magnificent houses in the whole of England! We are going to see pictures that surpass anything that is in the National Gallery or any other Museum!"

"The Marquis has invited you?" Nikola said.

"He has, as I told you, bought the Dughet from me. I hinted, just lightly of course, that I might have some other pictures which would interest him."

"Did he ask you where you got that one?"

"No, of course not," Jimmy said. "I told him I owned it and was only selling it because I was forced to do so."

He gave a little laugh before he said:

"He was so impressed when I described King's Keep to him that I know he will want to come here and look at it for himself."

"If he does, will he not realise it could not have come from here?"

"Why should he? I might have kept it in the cellar rather than with the family collection, and I assure you he will pay a very high price for anything else like it."

Jimmy was wildly excited by the large cheque he had brought home with him.

There was nothing Nikola could have done to dampen his spirits.

She only knew that she was worried.

She had what amounted to a presentiment.

It was that however genial the Marquis of Ridgmont

might appear to Jimmy, there was something sinister about him.

"I am just . . imagining . . it," she tried to tell herself.

At the same time, the feeling was there, and she was frightened.

CHAPTER TWO

Nikola was arranging some flowers when her brother came into the room.

"We are going tomorrow," he said, "to stay with Aunt Alice again.

"Aunt Alice?"

Nikola turned to stare at him in astonishment.

"That is what I said," Jimmy replied.

"But . . we have only just been there, and you know how you disliked the discomfort and the food."

"I am not going to give you three guesses why we are returning there," Jimmy said.

Nikola started.

"Oh, no, Jimmy!" she cried. "You cannot . . take any . . more of her . . pictures!"

"I have to have some by Friday," he replied, "to take to the Marquis."

Nikola put down the flowers.

She walked to where he was standing with his back to the mantelpiece.

"Now listen, Jimmy," she said. "We cannot . . go on like . . this!"

"We cannot go on without money," he replied. "I have given the order for the curtains and chairs. That will swallow up everything we have in the Bank."

"We can do . . without new curtains," Nikola said beneath her breath.

She knew it was hopeless arguing with her brother.

He would steal the Crown Jewels if it was for King's Keep.

She only thought despairingly that they were sinking further and further into crime.

"I want you to help me," Jimmy said in a determined voice, "and I wish to take Aunt Alice a present."

"I think she will be very surprised if you do so," Nikola retorted.

"It was something I should have thought of doing last time we went there," James went on in a lofty air. "In the East everybody always arrives with a present for their host."

"But we are not in the East . . although I agree it is a . . pleasant custom."

She looked at her brother.

She was wondering if she should go on pleading with him.

She wanted to go on her knees and beg him not to take anything more from that ugly house which depressed her.

She however knew he would not listen, so after a moment she said:

"I cannot imagine anything that Aunt Alice would like in the shape of a present considering, as you said yourself, that the house is full of treasures."

"I was not thinking of pictures or snuff-boxes," Jimmy replied, "but perhaps a dog."

"A dog?" Nikola exclaimed. "You must be crazy! It would need feeding and that would cost her money."

"Then what do you suggest?" Jimmy asked.

Jokingly Nikola said:

"Bessie has three kittens in the kitchen which she wishes to dispose of."

"Kittens!" Jimmy exclaimed. "That is a very good idea!"

"I do not think Aunt Alice would think so, even though they are exceptionally pretty kittens."

Jimmy walked out of the Drawing-Room and along the passage to the kitchen.

When he was gone, Nikola sank down in a chair.

"What am I to do?" she asked. "I know this is wrong, but because it is all for King's Keep, I do not believe a Regiment of soldiers could stop him!"

Every instinct in her body shrank from the idea of accepting their Aunt's hospitality again.

Even though it was reluctant, so that they could steal from her.

She wondered despairingly if there was anything she could do.

Jimmy came back into the room.

In his hands he was carrying a small white ball of fluff.

Despite herself, Nikola smiled.

"They really are very pretty!" she said. "And we cannot keep all three of them."

"Well, this one is going to Aunt Alice."

"I am sure she will refuse it."

"Then we will bring it back with us when we leave the next day," Jimmy said.

He was implying that they would have other things to bring back with them.

Nikola lapsed into silence.

Her brother put the kitten on the table.

It ran up and down looking very pretty as it did so.

"I will take a bet with you," Jimmy said, "that when she sees *Snowball* which is what I intend to call this kitten, Aunt Alice will fall in love for the first time in her life!"

"You are asking for a miracle," Nikola replied.

At the same time she was laughing because Jimmy made it sound so funny.

· · · · · ·

James and Nikola set off the next morning.

Snowball was in a basket which Nikola had padded with some old material in a pretty shade of pink.

She had also tied several bows of satin ribbon on the handle.

It made it look a very attractive gift.

They drove through the dusty lanes as they had done only a short time ago.

Nikola was wishing with all her heart that Jimmy had never realised how large their Uncle's collection of pictures was.

Only when they had driven for a long time in silence did she ask:

"What will you say if Aunt Alice tells you she has noticed that the picture you took was no longer there, and also the miniatures?"

"If you want the truth," Jimmy answered, "as it was the first time I had stolen anything, I was extremely foolish."

"In what way?" Nikola enquired.

"I should have taken a great deal more, and saved myself this second visit. This time, I do not intend to be so stupid."

The way he spoke made Nikola shiver.

She knew that he had every intention of filling the large trunk in which he had made her pack her clothes.

"It is far too big for one night," she had protested.

He did not bother to answer her.

She therefore included several starched petticoats she did not really need.

She knew that they could be crushed down to make room for the pictures.

But on their arrival the housemaids would not think it strange there was so much room in the trunk.

She always loved driving with her brother.

If their object had been different, she would have enjoyed seeing the countryside.

The Spring flowers in the hedgerows were very lovely.

But now, every minute took them nearer and nearer to their Aunt.

She therefore merely felt apprehensive. She was sure Lady Hartley would be suspicious because they had called again so soon.

As usual Jimmy had been determined to get his own way.

He had not given his Aunt a chance of saying that she did not want them.

He had merely, Nikola discovered, written her a letter saying that he was very anxious to see her again.

He hoped they could stay with her overnight.

Otherwise as she would understand, it would be tiring for the horses.

They drove up to the house.

It looked, Nikola thought, even uglier than she remembered.

There was a groom waiting outside with what she suspected was a surly expression on his face.

She thought, like the other servants, he would be resenting the extra work they made for him.

Jimmy, however, was charming to everybody.

He greeted the groom as if he was an old friend.

He told the Butler in his threadbare coat that he was delighted to see him again.

He smiled at the footmen.

Then they walked into the Drawing-Room where Lady Hartley was seated in her usual chair.

She looked, Nikola thought anxiously, very unwelcoming.

"Good-afternoon, Aunt Alice!" Jimmy said in his most

effusive manner. "It is delightful to see you again!"

"I am very curious as to why you are here," Lady Hartley said in an uncompromising voice.

"The answer is quite simple," Jimmy replied, "we have brought you a present."

As he spoke he deposited the basket containing *Snowball* at her feet.

"A present . . ?" Lady Hartley began.

Then she looked into the basket and asked:

"What is it?"

It is a kitten called *Snowball*," Jimmy replied. "I suddenly realised after we had left you that it was the one thing missing in the house."

But I do not like pets!" Lady Hartley said firmly.

At the same time she was looking down into the basket.

Snowball had slept peacefully while they were moving.

He was now standing with his paws on the side of the basket.

He looked very sweet against the pink background.

Neither Jimmy nor Nikola said anything.

Then after a moment Lady Hartley remarked:

"It is a pretty little cat. I have never seen a completely white one before."

"*Snowball* is unique," Jimmy said, "and that is exactly why, Aunt Alice, we wanted you to have him."

"I really do not think . . " Lady Hartley began.

Before she could finish the sentence, Jimmy took *Snowball* from the basket and placed him in her lap.

As if she could not help herself, Lady Hartley put out her hands to prevent the kitten from falling over and held him steady.

Then as *Snowball* began to purr, she said as if the words were dragged from her:

"It is certainly an attractive little creature!"

34

"That is exactly what I thought," Jimmy said with satisfaction, "and it will be company for you Aunt Alice."

Nikola was certain she would say she did not want company.

Then she realised her Aunt was not listening.

She was looking down at *Snowball* with an expression in her eyes Nikola had never seen before.

Jimmy glanced at her meaningfully.

It was no use! Jimmy was always right, and once again he had got his own way.

Butters came in with the usual minute glass of sherry.

Afterwards they went up to change for dinner.

By this time it was obvious that Lady Hartley was completely captivated by the new addition to her household.

"I told you so!" Jimmy said as they reached their bedrooms.

Nikola made a grimace at him, but she felt a little happier.

At least they had "given" something, which was better than just "taking".

. . . .

Later that night Jimmy came into Nikola's room carrying two pictures with him.

She was almost asleep.

She had guessed when she went to bed that he intended to visit the rooms that were shut up.

She had therefore left two candles burning.

Jimmy came into her bedroom.

She saw with relief that the pictures he was carrying were not very large.

He put one down on the bed.

"It is called *A Young Couple*," he said in a whisper, "and it is by Van Leyden."

It was not a particularly attractive picture, Nikola thought.

Yet she had heard her father mention the name of Van Leyden.

She was almost sure that he had been a pupil and admirer of Durer.

She did not speak, and Jimmy showed her the other picture.

"This is by Mabuse," he said, "who was a Flemish painter."

It was a clever portrait of a rather unattractive girl.

But Nikola could see that the gown was brilliantly painted.

So was the cap which haloed her hair and was set on the back of her head.

As if Jimmy was impatient at her not being more enthusiastic, he turned and went from the room.

He left the pictures on her bed. For a moment she could hardly believe he had gone.

Then she thought that as he had not said goodnight he would be returning.

"Surely," she said to herself, "he cannot be collecting any more?"

She got out of bed and put the two pictures into the bottom of her trunk.

She then began to repack the clothes which the house-maids had hung in the wardrobe.

She had not got very far before Jimmy returned.

"You have not . . taken any . . more?" she asked in a whisper.

It was a stupid question.

He was carrying what seemed to her much too large a picture.

He put it down on the bed.

By the light of the candles she could see that it really was very attractive.

36

"This is called *The Virgin in the Rose Garden*" Jimmy said, "and it is by Lochner. When the Marquis sees it, he will be absolutely delighted!"

"But . . it is . . too big!" Nikola complained.

"It will go into your trunk," Jimmy replied.

"Actually it is only about 20 inches high, but I cannot leave the frame behind."

"N.no . . of course . . not . . " Nikola stammered.

She thought her Aunt would be extremely suspicious if the frame was discovered without a picture in it. Jimmy walked across to her trunk. He removed the things she had packed.

Then he took out the two pictures which she had put at the bottom of it.

For a moment Nikola was not concerned with what he was doing.

She was thinking how lovely the picture was.

It was something she would love to own herself.

The Virgin with the Child Jesus on her lap was seated on a throne.

She wore a very elaborate silken gown billowing out in front of her.

In the background were a number of winged angels.

Two were in flight in the top corners of the picture.

The whole composition was lovely and perfectly executed.

She could understand Jimmy wanting to take it away.

It was, however, impossible to believe that anyone could lose such a treasure, and not be aware of it.

"I knew you would think it beautiful," Jimmy was saying as he came back to stand beside her.

"I am sure it is . . dangerous to . . steal it!" Nikola retorted.

"I doubt if Aunt Alice had any idea it was there," he answered. "You can see the dust is thick on the frame."

He picked up the picture as he spoke.

He carried it across the room and put it very carefully into the trunk.

With surprising skill for a man he packed some of her clothes on top of it.

Then he added the other two pictures.

Nikola was sitting on the bed in her nightgown.

As he finished she knew by the expression of satisfaction on his face how pleased he was with himself.

He came to her side.

"Get up early," he ordered, "and pack everything else before you are called!"

As Nikola did not say anything he went on:

"Fasten the two straps and be quite certain not to leave anything out so that the housemaids open the trunk again."

He was giving her orders, Nikola thought, as if she was a raw recruit.

She realised he was frightened of losing something that would be of such importance to King's Keep.

"All right, Jimmy," she replied in a whisper, "I will do as you say."

He smiled and kissed her.

"You are a good girl," he said. "Sleep well!"

He walked to the door.

He hesitated for a moment, just in case somebody might be in the passage.

She heard him go into his own room.

Then she went to her trunk.

She packed everything she possessed except for the gown she would wear tomorrow, and the nightgown she had on. She put her starched petticoats on top of the trunk.

When it was closed they would be crushed down.

She knew Jimmy was right.

It would be dangerous for a housemaid to see how full the trunk was compared with when she had unpacked it.

When Nikola went back to bed it was difficult to sleep.

She kept thinking how wrong it was to steal anything so beautiful as *The Virgin in the Rose Garden*.

There was something very spiritual about the picture.

She felt when she looked at it, that it vibrated towards her.

She was sure it was the Faith which had been poured into it by those who had worshipped in front of it over the years.

It had become Holy so that it could bless those who prayed to the Virgin.

Although the picture was now hidden in her trunk, Nikola found herself praying to the Virgin.

She asked Her to help Jimmy and prevent what he was doing from being discovered.

It was a very fervent prayer.

She could not help wondering how they could go on indefinitely.

Perhaps coming back again and again to steal pictures from Aunt Alice?

Then making another visit to Lord Mersey and anyone else who had valuable pictures.

"Help us please . . Help us," Nikola prayed.

She thought that the Mother of God holding the Holy Child heard her.

. . . .

Nikola was up and dressed by the time the maid came to call her at eight o'clock.

"You're early, Miss!" she remarked.

"We have a long way to go," Nikola replied, "and I have a lot of things to do when I get home."

The maid smiled.

"I 'spect they'll be waitin' for you," she said. "'Tis always th' same if one goes away. One comes back t' double what was there before one left."

"That is true," Nikola agreed.

She glanced round the room to be certain there was nothing left behind.

The straps on her trunk were secure, as Jimmy had ordered.

When she went downstairs to breakfast she found her Aunt already there. She was feeding *Snowball* with milk in a saucer.

"He slept on my bed all last night," she said to Nikola, "and never woke me once!"

She spoke in the voice of a mother who has just discovered her child is an infant phenomenon.

"I knew he was exactly what you wanted," Jimmy said with satisfaction, "and he will keep you free of mice."

"*Snowball* will have to grow a little first," Lady Hartley replied.

Almost for the first time since Nikola had known her, she laughed spontaneously.

She thought Jimmy had certainly made Aunt Alice happier than she had been before.

The world might think it a poor exchange.

A kitten whose value was practically nil for three masterpieces which were undoubtedly priceless.

But Nikola told herself, no one could put a price on happiness.

"Now remember, Aunt Alice," Jimmy was saying as they left, "*Snowball* should have fish to eat while he is so small, and chicken when he gets a little older."

"Yes, of course," Lady Hartley said, "and I am glad you reminded me."

"He will need a meal in the morning and a meal at night," Jimmy went on, "and I have never thought that rabbit is good for small cats."

Lady Hartley was hanging on his every word.

．　．　．　．　．　．　．

40

As Jimmy and Nikola drove away she asked:

"How is it you know so much about cats?"

"I do my home work, and I asked Bessie before we left what she gives our cat."

"I have to admit that I have never seen Aunt Alice look so human, or so happy!" Nikola said.

"I have my good points," Jimmy replied.

When they arrived home Jimmy cleaned the pictures as best he could.

He had learnt how to do so from one of the greatest experts in London.

Nikola looked at *The Virgin in the Rose Garden* every moment she had.

She knew that in two days time Jimmy would take it away.

Then she would never see it again.

She felt as if it spoke to her.

It made her feel not only that her prayers were heard, but that the Virgin was blessing her.

"I wish we could keep that picture," she said wistfully to Jimmy."

So do I," he agreed.

Nikola hesitated. Then she said:

"You do not suppose we could change it for one in the house which is not so beautiful? Or perhaps so valuable?"

Jimmy's lips were set in a hard line.

I stole this to save King's Keep," he said. "If I kept it for myself and for our pleasure, I should feel I was cheating!"

Nikola gave a little laugh.

"I suppose in a way, I understand your somewhat twisted principles." Jimmy did not reply, and she added:

"If I had enough money I would buy the picture from you."

"That is what the Marquis of Ridgmont will do!" Jimmy retorted.

Nikola knew it would be a long drive to the Marquis's house in Huntingdonshire.

They could have gone some of the way by train.

It would however, be much more difficult to convey the pictures that way than if they went by road.

Fortunately the two carriage-horses they possessed were young and strong.

As long as they had a good rest after they arrived, the journey would not hurt them.

It was on the Thursday before they left that Jimmy said:

"I suppose, really, I should have told you to buy a new gown to wear."

"A new gown?" Nikola repeated in astonishment.

"Well, the Marquis, being one of the wealthiest men in England, can afford to be very smart."

Nikola looked at him in consternation.

"Are you . . saying that the Marquis is . . young and that he may . . have a house-party?"

"I suppose he is about thirty-three or thirty-four," Jimmy replied, "and it is very likely he will be entertaining his friends."

"I . . I thought he would be . . old . . like Lord Mersey."

It was very stupid Nikola thought, but she had not expected a young man would be a fervent collector of pictures.

It had never struck her that they would not be alone with the Marquis.

It is what they had been with Lord Mersey.

Or else just a small family gathering.

"I had much better not come with you," she said quickly.

Jimmy stared at her.

"Do not be so ridiculous! How could I possibly manage without you?"

"I do not see why not. You are not going to steal from the Marquis, you are going to take him something!"

"I know that," Jimmy said, "but I want you to look sad when I say we must sell things from our own house. Also because you are so pretty, you may prevent our host from asking too many uncomfortable questions!"

Nikola stared at her brother in sheer astonishment.

"You have never said that before!"

"The Marquis of Ridgmont is rather different from the other people we have stayed with," Jimmy replied.

Then mockingly he added:

"I saw old Mersey, ancient though he is, eyeing you, and there is no doubt he thought you were just as attractive as the Venuses he had on his walls!"

Nikola laughed.

"Now you are making fun of the whole thing! At the same time, I have nothing new to wear."

"And I suppose there is no time to buy anything," Jimmy said reflectively.

"Not unless I fly to London on wings," Nikola replied, "or one of the ghosts in the house has a magic wand!"

Jimmy shrugged his shoulders.

"Very well, he will have to accept you as you are, but I wish I had thought of it before."

Nikola thought the same thing.

But she had seldom asked her brother for anything personal.

She knew he always felt she was spending money that should be used on King's Keep.

Now she went up to her bedroom to look at what was hanging in her wardrobe.

She realised how inadequate it was.

Because there had been no money for extravagances, she had made her own gowns.

She was very skilful, but the material had not been expensive.

She would not pretend to herself that she could compete with Frederick Worth.

She had read about him and the other great fashion designers in *The Ladies Magazine*.

"What shall I do?" she asked forlornly. She spoke in little above a whisper.

She was seeing the elegant full-skirted gown worn by *The Virgin in the Rose Garden*.

Her question became almost a prayer.

She was sure the Virgin understood how important it was that she should help her brother.

It was then she thought of the curtains which hung on one of the four-poster beds.

They had been chosen many years before by her mother.

They were pure silk and of the same turquoise blue as the scarab she had seen from Egypt.

"It has always been a lucky colour in the East," her mother had said, "and as your father has put in this room some of his more exotic pictures, I thought it appropriate."

It was a room they used for special guests.

Lately it had remained empty, simply because Jimmy had been unable to ask anyone of any importance to stay.

Nikola knew one curtain would make her a very beautiful evening skirt.

She could fashion herself a bustle and a very pretty bodice out of the other.

The whole question was, did she have the time?

She ran to the bedroom, to take down the curtains.

Then she went down the stairs to the kitchen.

Bessie was seated at the table shelling the young peas that had just been brought in from the garden.

44

"Mr. James has asked me to have a new gown to wear when we go to stay with a friend of his the day after tomorrow," she said.

"A new gown, Miss Nikola?" Bessie asked.

"An' where's the money t' come from for that, I'd like t' know!"

"I'm going to use the bed-curtains in the Blue Room," Nikola explained.

Bessie stared at her.

"Is there anyone in the village who could help me?" Nikola asked. "I can cut it out and, as you know, I can sew very quickly, but I do not think I could make a whole new gown in a day and a half!"

Bessie thought for a moment.

"There's Mrs. Gibbons at Honeysuckle Cottage," she said.

"Her made th' new altar cloth for th' Church an' her daughter, who's nigh on fifteen 'as done some repairs t'th' curtains in th' Vicarage."

"Thank you, Bessie," Nikola replied.

"Two hours later Nikola was cutting out the gown on her bedroom floor.

Mrs. Gibbons was arranging her sewing-basket in the window.

By the evening they had the gown tacked together.

By working the whole of the next day until dinner-time Nikola had her gown.

There was still quite a lot to do before the gown was finished to perfection.

But just to look at she had a gown which she thought was as smart as anything that might have come from Paris.

Certainly the colour became her.

Her hair was fair, but it had little touches of red in it, which seemed to be accentuated by the blue of the silk.

It made her skin look very white.

She had cut out the gown, following a photograph she had seen in a magazine.

It had been lent to her by the Vicar's wife.

When it was finished Nikola was rather afraid the décolletage was too low.

She therefore added, which again she had seen in a magazine, a little frill of the same satin round the neck.

It matched the bustle which was made of frill upon frill until it touched the floor.

"'Tis th' prettiest gown I've ever seen!" Mrs. Gibbons exclaimed when she tried it on. "'An' you looks like a picture in it, Miss Nikola, you do, really!"

"'Thank you, Mrs. Gibbons, and I only hope that is what my brother will think," Nikola replied.

It flashed through her mind that it was more important for the Marquis to think so.

Then she laughed at herself.

Whenever Jimmy spoke of him he had sounded very grand and very important.

He would hardly notice anyone as insignificant as herself.

Now she had learnt that he was different from what she had expected, she had asked questions.

She had discovered that far from being old, he was extremely athletic.

He raced his own horses in Steeple-Chases.

Also although Jimmy was rather vague about this, he was a well-known traveller.

"Where does he travel to?" Nikola asked.

"About the world," Jimmy answered vaguely.

"And he still has time to collect pictures?"

"He has one of the best collections in the whole of England!" Jimmy assured her.

"It was of course handed down to him through the generations."

46

"And he is adding to it?" Nikola asked.

"Obviously," her brother answered, "or we would not be going there!"

"And what else does he do?"

"Enjoys himself!" Jimmy answered. "As he can well afford to do!"

"But he is not married?"

Jimmy laughed.

He has sworn that is something he will never do."

"But . . why?" Nikola questioned.

"Surely he wants an heir to inherit his pictures?"

Jimmy shrugged his shoulders.

"I expect he has been crossed in love, or has an aversion to being shackled. Anyway he is a confirmed bachelor, so it is no use your 'setting your cap' at him!"

"I was not thinking of doing any such thing!" Nikola said crossly.

She was annoyed that Jimmy should say anything so vulgar.

She did not ask any more questions.

She thought when she was alone that the Marquis sounded very awe-inspiring.

At the same time almost inhuman.

"I wish we could go somewhere else," she said to herself.

She knew, however, that her brother was counting every second until he could be with the Marquis.

He was determined to obtain from him a very large sum of money to spend on King's Keep.

CHAPTER THREE

The guests at the luncheon party were beginning to look at the time.

The Marquis thought with relief that he would be able to leave.

It had in fact, been quite an interesting luncheon at the French Embassy.

He had met several friends.

Lady Lessington, with whom he was having an *affaire de coeur* came up to him to say in a low voice:

"Will you dine with me tomorrow evening, Blake? George is going to the country."

"Unfortunately, so am I," the Marquis replied.

He saw the look of disappointment in her beautiful eyes and said:

"But I will see you next week."

There was a smile on her lips as she moved away to thank her host and hostess for their hospitality.

The Marquis watched her go.

He thought that Lady Lessington was undoubtedly one of the most beautiful women in London.

At the same time, he was honest with himself.

The fire which had blazed between them was not burning as brightly as it had.

If there was one thing the Marquis disliked, it was a love affair which flickered away.

Then there was nothing left but a few dying embers.

His reputation for being ruthless came from the fact that the moment an affair began to pall he ended it.

Not only abruptly but sometimes brutally.

Something fastidious within him revolted at accepting anything but the best.

It was what he expected and sought for in everything.

He wanted his houses to be perfect, his estates to be an example to other Landlords!

Naturally his women must be uniquely beautiful.

He had managed through sheer cleverness not to be proclaimed a Roué as many of his friends were.

He was discretion itself.

He protected not only the reputation of the women whose favours he accepted, but also his own.

Lady Lessington left the large Salon, which was on the First Floor of the Embassy building, and descended the stairs.

As she did so the Marquis decided that he would not see her again.

Not intimately, although inevitably they would meet at parties and other functions.

He knew that she would resent and fail to understand his feelings about their affair.

But as he knew he was not her first lover, he was certain she would find another man to take his place.

At the same time he could not help knowing this would be difficult.

Without being conceited he was aware he was outstandingly handsome and also a very ardent lover.

He took as much trouble over his *affaires de coeur* as he did over his horses.

That was saying a great deal.

He climbed into his Chaise which was waiting for him outside and picked up the reins.

49

As he drove off he wondered, since he had finished with Lady Lessington, who next he would pursue.

She would leave a gap in his very full and busy life.

He needed to have a beautiful woman with whom he could relax.

What was more, he enjoyed the chase of some new and exotic Beauty.

It was in the same way as he enjoyed a good run on the hunting field, or riding in a hard Steeple-Chase in which he was invaribly the winner.

He vaguely remembered noticing a woman with the most striking red hair at Carlton House last night.

Her hair had struck him as being unusually lovely.

It was difficult now to recall her face.

He had no doubt she was beautiful.

He had only to ask the Prince of Wales, who had been their host, to learn who she was.

When he knew more about her he thought he might be disappointed.

For the moment however, it was something to look forward to.

The Marquis turned his horses at Hyde Park Corner towards Buckingham Palace.

He drove them with a flourish down the Mall.

They were a pair he had recently acquired from a friend.

He was an extravagant aristocrat who needed to raise a large sum of money immediately.

The two perfectly matched chestnuts had been, the Marquis thought, absurdly expensive.

At the same time, he had done his friend a good turn.

He therefore did not begrudge the money.

Anyway, the horses were worth it.

He realised a great number of people were admiring them as he drove down the Mall.

The top-hatted men and elegant women walking in the

Spring sunshine were staring not so much at himself as was usual, but at his horses.

They would, he thought, be an asset in his stables.

These already contained, in his opinion, the finest horses in England.

The same could be said of his race-horses which he stabled at Newmarket.

He remembered that he had two entered for the races which would take place next week.

He had not yet decided whom he would invite to his house-party there.

He was hoping, because he was not quite sure, that he had not included the Lessingtons.

It was something he would have to find out when he returned to his house in Park Lane.

His Secretary had a note of every invitation he had given or received for the next two months.

He drove across Horse Guards Parade thinking that was the simplest way of reaching Downing Street.

He had been an officer in the Household Cavalry.

He was therefore allowed to reach Whitehall through the gate which was guarded on each side by a trooper on horseback in a sentry-box.

From Whitehall he had only to turn right to be in Downing Street.

Now he began to wonder why the Prime Minister had sent for him.

It had been an urgent message which he could not ignore.

At the same time, it was inconvenient when he had other plans for the afternoon.

"I hope Lord Beaconsfield will not keep me long," the Marquis said to himself.

As a matter of fact he was always delighted to see Benjamin Disraeli who had been raised to the Peerage the year before.

51

The Marquis thought, as the Queen did, that he was undoubtedly the best Prime Minister England could have at the moment.

Her Majesty had a partiality for Lord Beaconsfield.

Although baptized into the Christian faith at the age of 13, he had been born into a Jewish family.

The Marquis was an astute man.

He had known that despite his eccentric appearance the Prime Minister was exactly the right man in the right place at the right time.

His brilliant brain, his wit and diplomatic tact had already proved him so, even to his critics.

The Marquis drove up to the door of Number 10.

He was shown into the Prime Minister's private Study.

Lord Beaconsfield rose from his desk to hold out his hand.

"I knew Your Lordship would not fail me," he said.

"That is something I hope I will never do!" the Marquis replied. "But of course I am wondering what catastrophe has occurred."

The Prime Minister laughed.

Coming from behind his desk he indicated an armchair in front of the fire.

It was quite a warm day.

There was however a fire burning and the Marquis knew that Lord Beaconsfield had a dislike of the cold.

He had noticed that his skin could look almost blue in the winter.

The draughts in the Houses of Parliament and the fogs coming up from the Thames could make the most warm-blooded Briton shiver.

The Marquis waited now while the Prime Minister put his long fingers together.

It was a characteristic gesture when he was thinking.

Finally he said:

"Her Majesty the Queen has become hysterical!"

If he had expected to shock the Marquis with his statement he did not succeed.

"I presume you are referring to the situation between Russia and Turkey, Prime Minister," he remarked.

Lord Beaconsfield's rather protruding lips twisted in a somewhat sarcastic smile.

"That is true," he answered. "We have been informed that the Russians have almost reached Adrianople, which is only 60 miles from Constantinople."

The Marquis raised his eye-brows.

"Have they really got as far as that?"

"There seems to be no reason to doubt the information," the Prime Minister replied, "and the Queen is furious! For months she has been trying to alert the Cabinet to the danger."

"I gather Turkey is not the main issue," the Marquis reflected. "It is really a question of Russian or British supremacy in the world."

"Exactly!" the Prime Minister agreed.

He gave a little laugh.

"I might have known, my dear Marquis, that you would know as much about the situation as I do!"

"You flatter me," the Marquis replied. "But I have been aware of the Queen's fears, and she was very voluble about them when I was last at Windsor."

The Prime Minister sighed.

"Confidentially she threatens to abdicate!"

The Marquis gave the Prime Minister a questioning look and he went on:

"This morning she has written to me saying:

'If England is to kiss Russia's feet, the Queen will not be a party to the humiliation of England and will lay down the crown!'"

"Strong words!" the Marquis remarked. "I very much

doubt, however, that Her Majesty would go as far as that!"

"She went on to say," Lord Beaconsfield added:

"'Oh, if the Queen were a man, she would like to go to give those horrid Russians, whose word cannot be trusted, a beating!'"

The Marquis laughed.

"She is magnificent!" he exclaimed. "If she was a man, she could not do better."

"I agree with you," the prime Minister replied. "But what Her Majesty wants at the moment, and so do I, is more information."

Lord Beaconsfield looked straight at the Marquis and there was a pause.

Finally the Marquis said:

"I am beginning to see where I come into this! What do you expect me to do?"

"What Her Majesty wants," the Prime Minister replied, "and what I also require, is first-hand information from somebody who is not already involved in this appalling situation."

"First-hand information!" the Marquis repeated. "How the devil do you suggest I am going to get it?"

Lord Beaconsfield bent forward in his chair.

"No-one, My Lord, is cleverer than you are at finding out the truth."

"I might have been fortunate enough to do that on several occasions in the past," the Marquis replied, "but this situation is very different because Britain is not involved."

"We may have to be," the Prime Minister said simply.

"In what way?" the Marquis enquired.

"We might have to make a show of strength when it is no longer a question of talking."

54

"What do you want me to do?" the Marquis asked in a resigned voice.

"What I want you to do is to go immediately on a secret mission," Lord Beaconsfield replied, "and find out everything you can."

"Just as simple as that!" the Marquis exclaimed mockingly, spreading out his hands in a somewhat theatrical gesture.

"I know it will not be easy," the Prime Minister admitted, "but the Queen trusts you, and so do I. You speak Russian, and you have an uncanny knack, as you well know, of getting to the root of a problem when everybody else fails."

The Marquis sighed.

"Do you want me to leave immediately?"

"Her Majesty has suggested, and I agree it is the best plan, that you should take the train to Athens," the Prime Minister said, "then cruise on your yacht towards Constantinople, making contact with a number of sources of information which are as well known to you as they are to the Foreign Office."

"I cannot think it will be a particularly pleasant journey you are suggesting to me!" the Marquis remarked.

He was thinking as he spoke of the discomfort of a long train journey across Europe.

As if he read his thoughts, Lord Beaconsfield smiled.

"Her Majesty thought the same, and she has very graciously offered you the Royal coaches which, as you know, are her private property."

The Marquis looked surprised and the Prime Minister went on:

"Her Drawing-Room and Sleeping cars are kept at the *Gare du Nord* in Brussels. They will be attached to the trains which will eventually take you from Ostend to Athens."

"I am of course, deeply honoured!" the Marquis said.

"You and Her Majesty must have been very confident that I would not refuse your suggestion of a quiet holiday in the Aegean Sea."

"You have never failed us yet," the Prime Minister said, "and I cannot believe you will do so now."

"Very well," the Marquis said, "and my yacht, as it seems you already know, is in harbour at Gibraltar."

"You can telegraph your Captain to proceed immediately to Athens," the Prime Minister said. "You should both arrive at about the same time."

"Thank you!" the Marquis said sarcastically. "Are you assuming that those who are interested will believe I am taking a holiday just by myself? I should have thought, unless my reputation has deteriorated very rapidly, that both the Russians and the Turks, if they are taking an interest, will find it highly suspicious!"

Lord Beaconsfield laughed.

"Neither Her Majesty nor myself would presume to choose your companions for you," he said. "But I cannot believe that with your reputation, as you have said, you will find it difficult to find some congenial companion with whom you would like to spend a week or two at sea!"

The Marquis did not reply.

He was thinking it somewhat impertinent of the Queen and the Prime Minister to discuss his love-affairs.

He never spoke of them himself, not even with his closest friends.

The Prime Minister's perception was very strong, and he knew exactly what the Marquis was thinking.

He therefore bent forward to say:

"We trust Your Lordship, and we rely on you, but you do realise we want no-one – and I mean no-one – to have any idea why your yacht should be steaming through the Dardanelles and perhaps making for the Black Sea."

"That will certainly make things difficult!" the Marquis agreed.

"It is of the utmost importance there should not be so much as a whisper," the Prime Minister said. "If the gossips were aware of how concerned Her Majesty is about the Russian advance and the Turkish weakness, you know how dangerous they could be."

"What you are really saying," the Marquis replied, as if he was working it out for himself, "is that women talk, however much you tell them not to."

"That is true of most women," the Prime Minister agreed, "and therefore you must find one you can trust."

There was a twinkle in his eye as he said:

"Her Majesty has in fact, said it is a pity you have not a wife."

The Marquis threw up his hands in horror.

"If you and Her Majesty are going to combine in trying to press me into losing my freedom, I shall leave for America!"

The Prime Minister laughed.

"You know, My Lord, you would do nothing so drastic as that! At the same time, be careful whom you choose for, as you are aware, women not only listen on the pillow, but also talk on it!"

The Marquis rose to his feet.

"I can only say that you and Her Majesty are straining my patriotism to breaking-point!"

"On the contrary, we are paying you a very high compliment by sending you on this mission, because we know that no-one else has any chance of being successful."

"I am listening to your honeyed tongue, Prime Minister like a mesmerised rabbit!" the Marquis retorted.

Both men were laughing as they walked towards the door.

"Papers, maps and a new code will be at your house this evening," Lord Beaconsfield said.

The Marquis put out his hand, and Lord Beaconsfield took it in both of his.

"I can only thank you from the very bottom of my heart," he said very sincerely. "I am, as you well know, deeply concerned about the situation which is very different from what I say in public."

"I can only hope I do not fail you," the Marquis answered.

. . . . . .

Driving home, the Marquis thought that what he had been told to do was something he had never anticipated.

The situation in Eastern Europe had been played down in the newspapers.

Most people in England were not particularly interested.

The Tsar of Russia, Alexander II, had hoped that a recent Conference in Constantinople would provide a peaceful solution.

But the Sultan of Turkey had rejected everything that was suggested.

To the astonishment of the world, two weeks later the Tsar announced that his patience was exhausted and declared war on Turkey.

The majority of people in England including the Members of Parliament remained unmoved.

Both countries seemed a long way away.

If they fought amongst themselves and in their own lands, it did not concern Britain or her possessions elsewhere.

It was like the Queen, the Marquis thought, to be aware before anybody else that Russian supremacy in the Middle East could, in fact, be a great threat to Britain.

By the time he reached his house in Park Lane he had already decided that he could not leave England until Sunday.

He had a great many things to arrange and a large number of appointments to cancel.

Actually he had no wish to go away at this particular moment.

At the same time, something new, something unexpected, was always a challenge.

He could not help wondering whether this adventure, like so many others before would prove dangerous.

Having arrived at Ridge House he sent for his Secretary.

Mr. Grey was a middle-aged man who was as efficient as he was himself.

In a few short words he told him where he had to go and where the yacht was to meet him.

Mr. Grey took down a note of everything he said.

"You will be going to the country today, My Lord," he asked, "as was planned?"

"Yes, of course," the Marquis said. "There are a number of things I want to do at Ridge before I leave."

"You have not forgotten that you have invited Sir James Tancombe and his sister Miss Nikola Tancombe to stay?"

"No, I want to see Sir James," the Marquis replied. "I suppose I have invited some other guests?"

"Lady Sarah Languish, whom Your Lordship will remember invited herself, and on Your Lordship's instructions I asked Lord and Lady Cleveland and Captain Barclay for the weekend."

The Marquis sighed.

For a moment he had forgotten the house-party.

But Grey had arranged everything and at least they would prevent him from worrying unduly about what lay ahead.

"I suppose we shall have something to do on Saturday?" he asked tentatively.

"I thought Your Lordship would wish to try out the

new horses that recently arrived from Ireland, and I think Mr. Gordon has planned a small dinner on Saturday night."

It was the way in which the Marquis always entertained his guests.

He therefore nodded, knowing that the details would be carried out perfectly by Grey in London and his counterpart Gordon in the country.

He decided that the main thing would be to get on with the task that had been set him by the Prime Minister.

"I suppose," he said, "it will be possible for me to go abroad on Sunday, and my guests can either go then or stay on until Monday."

"Of course, My Lord," Mr. Grey replied. "I am sure the Prime Minister's secretary will have already alerted Brussels that Her Majesty's coaches will be required? Your Lordship will perhaps find the cross-Channel Steamer less crowded than on an ordinary week-day."

"Very well," the Marquis agreed. "I leave on Sunday morning, and I will of course take Dawkins with me."

Dawkins was his valet who had been his batman when he was in the Household Cavalry.

He was, the Marquis knew, invaluable when he was on a secret mission.

He was quite unperturbed by whatever dangers they encountered at such times.

At four o'clock precisely he boarded his private train which was waiting for him at St. Panrcas Station.

At five thirty it drew up at his private Halt which was only two miles from Ridge.

The Marquis's party from London was accommodated in a private coach which had been attached to another train which left a little earlier.

They were looked after by the Marquis's own servants, and supplied with tea or champagne, whichever they wanted.

The Marquis preferred travelling by himself.

He found the chatter of his guests before they finally arrived in the country spoilt his pleasure in welcoming them to his home.

The first time most people saw Ridge they were stunned by its appearance in the same way as they were overcome by the Marquis himself.

Ridge was enormous but architecturally perfect.

It had been built on a high piece of ground so that from the windows there was a fine view in all directions.

Since they lived in the country James and Nikola had not been asked if they wished to travel to Ridge by train.

They could, as the Marquis was well aware, easily arrive by road.

They had been informed by Mr. Grey that they would be expected any time after six o'clock, and Jimmy had been determined they would not be late.

It had, however, taken them longer than they had anticipated.

He actually turned in at the very imposing drive-gates of Ridge just on twenty minutes past six.

It was Nikola who was overcome first by the beauty of the drive.

The branches of the trees which bordered it met over-head so that they made a green archway.

Then as she saw the house she was speechless.

Never had she imagined a house could be so beautiful.

With hundreds of windows shining in the setting sun it looked like a Palace in a Fairy Tale.

"It is lovely, Jimmy," she exclaimed, "and so enormous! How can one man live in it all alone?"

"The Marquis is not often alone," Jimmy replied.

"I do hope there will not be too many other guests," Nikola said quickly. "I have only one decent gown with me."

"Then you had better wear it this evening," Jimmy replied. "First impressions are important."

Nikola wondered whom she was meant to impress.

She had already made up her mind that nothing she did or said, or the way she looked, would impress the Marquis.

Now she saw his house she knew that he would be surrounded like a hero in a novel by brilliant, intelligent and beautiful women.

Beside them she would be utterly insignificant.

Living alone at King's Keep when she was not helping in the house, she often sat reading in the garden.

The one thing that her mother had insisted upon was that they should have a large Library.

While her father had thought only of his pictures, her mother had bought books.

"We may not be able to afford to travel, dearest," she had said to her daughter, "but that need not make you feel restricted."

Nikola looked at her wide-eyed.

"Why not, Mama?"

"Because, my dearest, you can travel in your mind, and although you may not actually see the countries about which you are reading, you can imagine them, and understand why the people in them behave as they do."

It was something which Nikola began to enjoy when she was very small.

As she grew older books became part of her very breathing.

She quickly learned the languages of the countries in which she was interested.

Her mother found in the village a Frenchwoman who taught her French.

Then there was a School teacher who was proficient in Italian.

He had spent his childhood in that country.

62

Her education, Nikola thought when she was older, was almost like picking up jewels in a sandy desert.

It would seem there was nothing there.

Then suddenly, quite unexpectedly, there would be a glittering stone.

It turned out to be someone who was ready to teach her Spanish.

Then when she least expected it, she met a Russian girl.

She was a pupil at the School where Nikola attended daily in the Market Town only two miles from Kings Keep.

Her father would drive her there in the morning.

He would then fetch her back in the evening.

In three years she learnt really very little she did not already know.

The exception was the amount of languages she assimilated.

The Russian girl was the daughter of a Diplomat who had incurred the wrath of the Tzar.

He was therefore afraid to go back to Russia.

He settled with very little money in a rather dilapidated house in the Town.

He was a distinguished man and a Count.

Therefore the School which Nikola attended had agreed to educate his daughter for a very small fee.

Even that was more than he could really afford.

He and his family existed on what he could earn by writing articles on Russia.

He also wrote poems which no publishers wanted.

Nikola read them and found them very moving.

She became friends with Natasha.

Because Lady Tancombe felt sorry for the girl she frequently had her to stay at King's Keep.

She was beautiful in her own way.

She was very anxious to learn English.

Nikola was equally anxious to learn Russian.

They took it turn and turn about to teach each other.

Tzar Alexander II finally relented.

He forgave Natasha's father for whatever sin it was he had committed.

Then the family were able to return to Russia.

The two girls said goodbye to each other, both of them in tears.

"I shall never see you again," Natasha sobbed, "but I will always remember you, Nikola."

"As I shall remember you," Nikola said. "So please write to me sometimes, and tell me what you are doing."

They hugged each other.

Natasha went away and Nikola knew, although she did not say so, that something dreadful would happen to her.

It was two years before they learned what it was.

The whole family when they arrived in St. Petersburg had, through some whim or some twist in the Tzar's mind, been banished to Siberia.

The news made Nikola hate Russia and Russians.

She could only pray that she would never come in contact with such terrible people.

She was, of course, not thinking of Russia when she reached Ridge.

She was thinking that only in England could any house look so majestic and not be a Royal Palace.

When she first saw the Marquis she thought he should at least be a Prince.

Because of his good looks and his presence he seemed to stand out from the rest of the party.

On their arrival Jimmy and Nikola had been taken by what seemed to be an Army of servants up to their rooms.

It was suggested they might like to rest after their journey.

There was time before they changed for dinner.

Nikola was shown into a bedroom so beautiful that she felt it would be impossible to sleep in it.

Her brother's room was almost equally impressive.

It was connected to a *Boudoir* they shared.

Nikola was offered tea.

She felt shy of giving so much trouble to the servants and refused.

Only when the footman had shut the door did Jimmy, who was in the *Boudoir* say:

"Do not be so stupid! Accept everything you are offered. You are not likely ever to stay anywhere as grand as this again!"

"I am . . overwhelmed by it all!" Nikola said. "And everything is . . so beautiful!"

"Especially the pictures," Jimmy said.

There were certainly a lot of them on the walls.

"How can he possibly want any more when he has so many already?" Nikola asked.

"He is a Collector, thank goodness!" Jimmy explained. "And because he is a Collector, he will not be able to resist the pictures I have brought with me."

Nikola sighed.

"Oh, Jimmy, it would be so lovely if we were here just for ourselves, and did not have to be frightened in case he is suspicious as to where you got the pictures."

Jimmy laughed.

"When you have met the Marquis, you will find it impossible to imagine him sniffing around the closed up, dusty rooms in Aunt Alice's house!"

Nikola laughed because it sounded so funny.

"Now do stop worrying!" Jimmy snapped. "We are perfectly safe, and all I ask is that I leave here with a large cheque which will all be spent on King's Keep."

That was the only thing that made what they were doing acceptable, Nikola thought for the thousandth time.

When she returned to her bedroom, she found that everything had been unpacked.

She hoped the maid who waited on her had noticed her new gown.

She would certainly be surprised at the other two she had been obliged to bring with her.

She had been trying for months to save a little out of the money Jimmy gave her for the Housekeeping to buy a new day dress.

He had been obliged to buy her a coat for the Winter.

Otherwise, she thought, she would have frozen to death.

But he had grumbled endlessly at the extravagance.

Next Winter, Nikola told herself, she would wear the rugs off the floor rather than ask him for a single penny.

He had received a lot of money for the pictures and bowls he had stolen.

Yet he had not offered her any of it for herself.

He had however, slightly increased the amount she could spend on food.

Yet even if he had offered her some, she was determined to say 'No'.

At the same time, she was wondering how long her shoes would last.

Although she could make her own gowns, stockings and gloves had to be bought.

She had worn out practically everything that had belonged to her mother.

She knew that to a man she might look all right.

A woman would realise at once how shabby her clothes were.

"Anyway," she told herself cheerfully, "I will wear my new gown this evening, and if His Lordship has to see it again tomorrow, he will just have to think that his eyes are deceiving him!"

It all seemed ridiculous!

She was laughing as she started to undress.

Never in her life had she felt so lapped in luxury as she did when her bath was prepared for her in front of the fire.

There were two maids to bring in the hot and cold water.

It came in cans that were polished so highly that she could see her face in them.

'This is an adventure like those I have read about,' she thought.

Then she tried the temperature of the water with her foot.

CHAPTER FOUR

The Marquis did not greet his guests as he usually did immediately on their arrival.

He had too many important instructions to give to his Secretary.

He also had to have a consultation with Dawkins his valet, as to what clothes he would require for the journey.

By the time that he learned that all his guests had arrived it was time for him to dress for dinner.

He therefore went straight to his bedroom.

It was only while he was putting on his evening-clothes that he remembered Lord Beaconsfield had advised him to take some companion with him in his yacht.

He knew the only woman he could possibly ask would be Lady Sarah Languish.

She among all the Beauties he had courted recently was unencumbered by a husband.

Lady Sarah was the daughter of the Duke of Dorset.

She had been married when she was very young to a handsome, raffish and more or less impoverished aristocrat.

It had been considered quite a good match from the point of view of status.

The engagement was announced.

The Duke conferred with his future son-in-law's father about the Marriage Settlement.

It was then he realised how very little money there was.

It was too late for him to refuse to allow the marriage to take place.

He could only regret that his very beautiful daughter had not chosen a more eligible husband.

Sarah, who was only just eighteen, was quite understandably wildly in love with Ronald Languish.

He was ten years older than she was and very attractive.

He found her entrancing.

He also enjoyed riding the Duke's horses and staying in the Duke's houses.

When however they were alone in a not very comfortable home of their own, the glamour of their wedding began to fade.

Sarah had been very spoilt by her parents.

She was annoyed when she could not have as many servants as she wanted, better horses and most of all, expensive gowns.

Within a year they began to bicker at each other. Two years after the marriage had taken place they were more or less living separate lives.

It was, as far as Sarah was concerned, the greatest good fortune when Ronald Languish lost his life in a Steeple Chase.

He was riding a horse that was not capable of taking the high jumps that had been erected.

Falling at the third fence, he broke his spine.

Had he lived he would have been a helpless cripple.

The Duke sighed with relief that his daughter was now free.

Lady Sarah had no intention of marrying again.

She enjoyed herself with lover after lover, and at the same time became more beautiful.

She was one of the first of the beautiful women whom the public stood on the seats in Hyde Park to see drive by in her open Victoria.

Lady Sarah met the Marquis.

It was then she decided she would acquiesce in her father's pleading to marry for the second time.

The Marquis as a man was everything she desired.

His wealth and possessions were everything she wanted.

She pursued him relentlessly, but cleverly.

By that time she was far too experienced to make it at all obvious either to the gossips or to him what she intended. She swore, however, that he would be hers.

No one should take him from her.

She was not perturbed by his affair with Lady Lessington. Lord Lessington was in excellent health and Her Ladyship would never face the scandal of a divorce.

Lady Sarah just waited for her opportunity.

She heard from William that he had been invited to Ridge.

She knew this was her chance.

Without appearing to be particularly interested, she enquired of Willie:

"Is it a large party:"

"No, I do not think so," Willie replied. "Only the Clevelands and myself. We are going to try out some of the new horses that Blake has brought, and which he is certain will be the envy of all his friends!"

"That is nothing unusual," Lady Sarah remarked with a laugh.

She, however, had the information she wanted.

The Marquis had invited only a few friends for the week-end, and Lady Lessington was not among them.

She waited until she knew the Marquis would not be at home.

Then she called at his house in Park Lane and asked to see his Secretary.

Mr. Grey came hurrying into the Library into which she had been shown.

Lady Sarah smiled at him.

"Good-morning," she said. "I hear His Lordship is out."

"His Lordship will not be back until this afternoon," Mr. Grey replied.

"Then will you ask him if I can come to Ridge on Friday night and stay until Sunday? I have an engagement in the neighbourhood, and it would be very convenient if His Lordship would let me stay with him."

"I will give His Lordship your message, My Lady, as soon as he returns."

"Thank you," Lady Sarah said, "and if you could send a message to my house, I will be very grateful."

"I will do so immediately I have seen His Lordship, so Your Ladyship should know by this evening."

"You are very kind," Lady Sarah said in a soft voice which all men found fascinating.

She smiled at Mr. Grey and left.

He thought as she did so that she was very lovely.

He was certain his Master thought the same.

At the same time one could never be certain.

As he went back to his office Mr. Grey was thinking of the large number of beautiful women.

All of them had lasted only a short time before the Marquis became bored.

"I wonder what he really wants?" Mr. Grey questioned as he sat down at his desk. Then he told himself that it was none of his business.

. . . .

The Marquis had finished dressing.

He was thinking that if he was going to take Lady Sarah with him on Sunday, he would have to invite her tonight or first thing tomorrow morning.

He was quite certain she would not refuse.

But he supposed any woman would want at least twenty-four hours notice in order to see to her packing.

71

Doubtless she would want to buy a number of quite unnecessary extras before she undertook such a long journey.

As far as he was concerned, she would help the time to pass when they were in the train.

She would also be a perfect cover if anyone was curious as to why he should cruise from Greece along the coast of Bulgaria.

He took one quick glance at himself in the mirror to see that his tie was straight.

Then he proceeded down the wide corridor which led to the top of the stairs.

He was still thinking of Lady Sarah.

At the same time his eyes were searching the hall beneath him.

Two footmen were very smart in the Ridge livery.

The Butler, his hair just turning white, was waiting to direct the guests into the Drawing-Room.

There were the flags which hung on each side of the marble fireplace.

His ancestors had won them in various battles, in which inevitably the British had been the victors.

As he descended the staircase he glanced also at the pictures.

They had hung in the same place on the walls for over a hundred years.

It was then he remembered with a feeling of elation that Sir James Tancombe was bringing him some more pictures.

He hoped they were as good as the *Duchet*.

If so they would be exactly what he required for the new Gallery he had created in the East Wing.

The original Picture Gallery was full – his father had seen to that!

The new one had involved making several rooms into one large one.

72

The Marquis was determined that the paintings would be as distinctive and prestigious as those collected by his forebears.

He entered the Drawing-Room to find some of his guests already there.

There were Lord and Lady Cleveland, who were distant cousins of whom he was very fond, and Lady Sarah.

They were all laughing as he proceeded towards them.

Then when they saw him Lady Cleveland rose to her feet.

"Blake, how lovely to see you!" she said as he kissed her. "You know how I adore being at Ridge, which is looking even more beautiful than when I last saw it."

"That is what I like to hear," the Marquis replied with a smile.

He shook hands with Lord Cleveland saying:

"I have been looking forward to seeing you, Arthur."

Then he turned to Lady Sarah.

She was deliberately standing a little to one side.

It was so that he could admire her before he actually reached her.

When he did she held out both her hands.

"Have you forgiven me for thrusting myself upon you?" she asked.

"You know without my saying so," the Marquis replied, "that you are always welcome at any time."

He saw the expression in her eyes and knew how the evening would end.

As if with an effort the Marquis turned back to the Clevelands.

"What were you laughing about when I came into the room?" he asked. "I feel I missed something amusing."

"Very amusing," Lady Cleveland answered.

"Sarah was telling us a very naughty story about George

73

Hamilton, but we have been sworn to secrecy, so I must not repeat it!"

"Except of course, to me!" the Marquis said lightly.

Even as he spoke it flashed through his mind that Lady Sarah should not gossip about the Duke of Hamilton.

He was an older and highly respected man.

If she could gossip about him she might easily do so about other people on matters which Lord Beaconsfield had impressed on him no one must ever mention.

The door of the Drawing-Room opened.

"Sir James Tancombe and Miss Nikola Tancombe, my Lord!" the Butler announced.

The Marquis turned round.

Coming towards him was Nikola wearing the turquoise blue gown she had made herself.

She could not have known that the Drawing-Room was a perfect background for it.

The walls were white picked out with gold leaf.

The Louis XIV chairs and sofas were covered in an almost identical blue to the gown she was wearing.

Everything in the room had been chosen to blend with the furniture.

Even the carpet, was predominantly blue and white.

As she moved towards the Marquis, he thought she was like a piece of the Sèvres porcelain which stood on the mantelpiece.

She also resembled a picture by Boucher in which was incorporated exactly the same shade of blue.

He shook hands first with James.

"It is nice to see you again, Sir James!" the Marquis said. "I am so glad you persuaded your sister to come with you."

Nikola dropped the Marquis a very graceful curtsy.

Then as he took her hand in his he was aware that her fingers were trembling.

It was as if he held a small and frightened bird captive.

74

As he looked into her eyes, which were large and seemed to dominate her face, he knew again that she was afraid.

Because he wished to reassure her, he held her fingers for a little longer than was necessary.

Then he said:

"Come to meet my friends. We are a very small party."

While he was performing the introductions, Captain Barclay came hurrying into the room.

"I am not late, am I?" he said to the Marquis. "I lost my shirt-stud and had to borrow one of yours."

Lady Cleveland teased him for being so careless and he greeted Lady Sarah.

The Marquis then introduced him to Nikola and James.

He stared at her in astonishment.

"Why have I not met you before?" he asked. "Where have you been hiding:"

"Where I live," Nikola replied, "in the country."

"It is a place called 'King's Keep'," Lady Cleveland interposed. "I have already heard a great deal about it from our host."

"It sounds enchanting," Willie said.

"That is what all the Tancombes think it is," Nikola answered, "but of course, they are prejudiced!"

She found William Barclay easy to talk to.

She was glad she was sitting next to him at dinner.

The Marquis had Lady Cleveland on his right, and Lady Sarah on his left.

It was some time before Nikola was brave enough to look at him again.

She thought that he was even more autocratic and frightening than she had expected him to be.

Sitting at the head of the table, in a carved armchair made in the reign of Charles II, he looked Royal.

At the same time he was vibrant in a way she could not explain to herself.

Jimmy had told her how the Marquis expected perfection.

She decided that he must be very perceptive.

If he was, he was therefore, dangerous.

She thought as she glanced at him at dinner that he had what her father had called an "eagle eye".

"Eagles can see further than other birds," he explained, "and they miss very little. The smallest mouse or rabbit hundreds of feet below them cannot escape."

"He is dangerous! He is dangerous!"

Nikola could feel the words repeating themselves in her mind.

All the time she was talking to Willie, or to Lord Cleveland, who was on her other side, she was pulsatingly aware of him.

The dinner was superb, and so were the wines that accompanied it.

The conversation was witty and amusing.

Because the party was so small they talked across the table as well as to those on each side of them.

In fact, Nikola would have thought it was the most entertaining meal she had ever had.

But there was something like a stone in her breast, which she knew was fear.

"I am being ridiculous!" she told herself as the ladies left the gentlemen to their port. "Why should the Marquis be suspicious of anything Jimmy offers him?"

She looked at the pictures in the corridor along which they were walking.

She knew those that were hanging in the Drawing-Room would have thrilled her father.

"Why should the Marquis want more?" she asked angrily.

"Come and tell me about yourself, Miss Tancombe," Lady Cleveland said kindly.

She was a very considerate person.

She thought perhaps a girl who was so much younger than the rest of the party might be feeling a little shy.

Nikola sat down beside her on the sofa.

"I am overcome by this magnificent house!" she said.

"That is what we all feel when we come to Ridge!" Lady Cleveland laughed.

"I expect its owner is tired of being told how wonderful it is, almost as if it was not real," Nikola answered.

Lady Cleveland smiled.

"On the contrary, I think he expects the compliments, and would be surprised and perhaps irritated if they were not forthcoming."

"My brother is the same," Nikola said. "He thinks King's Keep is perfect, and is astounded if people are not wildly enthusiastic as soon as they see it."

"I suppose most men are like that," Lady Cleveland replied. "Where my husband is concerned, it is horses, and the first thing you have to inspect when you stay with us, is the stables!"

Nikola laughed.

She was feeling less tense because Lady Cleveland was so kind.

The gentlemen came to join them.

The Marquis noticed as he entered the room that the usual card-tables had been erected at one end of it.

He walked up to Lady Cleveland.

"I know, Iris," he said, "you are longing to play Bridge, and Willie and Lady Sarah will join you."

Lady Sarah, who had risen when he came into the room put her hand on his arm.

"I want to play with you," she said softly.

"Perhaps later," the Marquis replied. "I intend now to take Sir James and his sister to my Study. We will not be long, then perhaps we can have a few hands of Baccarat."

Lady Sarah looked disappointed.

Nikola felt as if the stone in her breast was almost too heavy to be borne.

She was aware, however, there was a light in Jimmy's eyes.

As they walked out of the Drawing-Room with the Marquis he asked:

"Shall I go to fetch the pictures I have brought you? They are upstairs in my bedroom."

"A footman could do that for you," the Marquis replied, "although I expect you would rather carry them yourself."

Jimmy walked towards the stairs and the Marquis said to Nikola:

"We go this way."

They walked down the corridor in the opposite direction from the one they had taken to the Dining-Room.

The Marquis took Nikola into a room which she thought was exactly what a man's Study should look like.

The walls were covered in sporting pictures and over the mantelpiece there was a magnificent painting of a horse by Stubbs.

The sofa and chairs were covered in dark red leather.

As they entered, two spaniels rose from the hearth-rug to greet the Marquis.

There was a flat-topped writing-desk with gold feet and handles.

It had been made in the reign of George III.

A glass-fronted Chippendale cabinet was filled with a number of handsomely bound books.

The red velvet curtains matched the colour of the sofa and chairs.

Nikola thought that once again the Marquis had attained perfection.

"Do sit down, Miss Tancombe," he said, "and I hope you enjoyed your dinner."

"I can say in all honesty that it was the best dinner I have ever eaten," Nikola replied, "but I am finding your house so breath-taking that it is difficult to think of anything else."

"That is what I like to hear," the Marquis said. "At the same time it worries me that you look frightened."

Nikola looked away from him towards the fire.

It was not what she expected him to say, and she therefore had no answer.

"You are very beautiful," the Marquis remarked, "and it is therefore wrong that you should look anything but happy."

She was so astonished at the compliment that she turned to look at him.

Then as her eyes met his she felt the colour flooding into her cheeks.

She looked away again.

"Is it possible," the Marquis asked, "that you find my compliments embarrassing?"

"It . . it is something to . . which I am . . not accustomed," Nikola replied.

"Is King's Keep in the middle of the desert, or are all the men in the neighbourhood blind?" the Marquis enquired.

Nikola laughed.

"It is not as bad as that, but I do not see many young people. James's friends are so intent on admiring the house and the pictures that they rarely look at me!"

The Marquis laughed.

"That is certainly a very sad story!"

He paused before he added:

"When you came into the Drawing-Room this evening wearing a gown which might have been designed at the same time as the room itself, I thought I must be dreaming."

"Now you . . mention it . . I realise my gown is the . . same colour as the china . . and these . . beautiful French chairs."

"Exactly!" the Marquis said. "And perhaps when you bought it, you had a presentiment that you would wear it in this house."

Nikola thought the Marquis would be surprised if he knew she had made the gown herself, and in one-and-a-half days.

However she did not have to answer.

At that moment the door opened and Jimmy came in carrying the pictures.

As usual, when Jimmy was doing anything special for King's Keep he became more animated.

It was as if his whole being lit up.

He spoke not only with his mind, but also with his heart and soul.

He was speaking of the thing he loved best in the world.

The Marquis sat down in an armchair.

He looked, Nikola thought, like Jupiter, King of the Gods, condescending to the mere mortals beneath him.

Jimmy showed him first of all the Van Leyden.

He was clever enough to let the Marquis see for himself the colours of the man's strangely shaped hat and the question in the girl's eyes as she looked at him.

The Marquis did not say anything, and Jimmy then produced the Mabuse.

"This is surely Mabuse," he said.

Now the Marquis sat forward in his chair and exclaimed:

"It is a portrait of Jacqueline de Bourgogne. How on earth did you come by that?"

"I am not certain from where my father obtained it," Jimmy replied vaguely, "but I think it is the most perfect example of his brilliant technique."

"I agree with you!" the Marquis replied.

Then with the air of a magician about to perform his *pièce de résistance*, Jimmy produced *The Virgin in the Rose Garden*.

80

He propped it against a chair.

The Marquis stared at it.

"A Lochner!" he exclaimed.

"One of the best examples of his work," Jimmy said, "and my sister can hardly bear to part with it."

The Marquis looked at Nikola.

Her eyes were on the painting.

Once again she was praying to the Virgin for help.

There was silence until the Marquis said:

"I think, Tancombe, I should thank you for bringing me three remarkable pictures which I shall certainly be proud to have in my collection."

"I was sure that was what you would feel about them," Jimmy said. "Especially the Lochner."

"It is exquisite!" the Marquis agreed. "I know that once it is mine I shall never want to part with it."

"That is what I feel myself," Jimmy agreed. "At the same time, there is so much to be done at King's Keep, and repairs, as we all know, cost money."

Quite suddenly Nikola felt she could not bear to hear her brother talking like that.

She also knew that they would soon be negotiating over the price.

She felt that to think of *The Virgin in the Rose Garden* in terms of money was an insult.

Nothing so beautiful or so Holy could ever be assessed in pounds, shillings and pence.

She rose to her feet.

"Will you . . forgive me . . My Lord," she said in a very small voice, "if I . . retire to bed? I have a . . slight headache after . . the journey."

"But of course," the Marquis said. "I quite understand, and as it is Friday night, none of us will stay up late."

"Thank you."

She walked towards the door.

Before she could reach it the Marquis was there before her.

He held it open.

"I trust you will sleep well," he said in his deep voice.

Nikola made an effort to smile at him then without replying she moved away down the corridor.

She heard the door close behind her.

The Marquis had gone back and now the bargaining for the pictures would commence.

She was well aware that Jimmy would start by asking a far higher sum than he expected to get.

"If only we could have kept *The Virgin in the Rose Garden*, she told herself, "then I am sure our troubles would have been at an end."

She knew by the expression on the Marquis's face that he had been surprised that Jimmy would sell such a magnificent picture.

Any connoisseur and Collector would want to keep it for himself.

It would have been better, Nikola thought, if Jimmy had brought away something less important.

But it was too late for regrets.

She reached her bedroom.

Because she was inexperienced in staying in grand country houses, she did not ring for the maid to help her undress.

She hung her gown up in the wardrobe.

As she did so she thought how the Marquis had complimented her on its colour.

It was strange that the curtains in the Blue Room at King's Keep should exactly match the Drawing-Room at Ridge.

"That was certainly something Mama did not anticipate when she hung them Nikola thought.

She got into bed, but it was impossible to sleep.

She could only lie worrying about what was happening downstairs.

She wondered what payment Jimmy had obtained from the Marquis.

It was two hours later when he opened the communicating-door from the Boudoir and peeped in.

"Are you awake?" he whispered.

Nikola sat up in bed.

One candle was still alight because she had been almost sure Jimmy would come to tell her what had happened.

He walked towards the bed and sat down facing her.

"What do you think I got?" he asked.

"I cannot imagine," Nikola replied.

"Ten thousand pounds!"

Nikola gave a little cry and put her hands up to her face.

"I . . I do not believe . . it!"

"I can hardly believe it myself," Jimmy said.

"It must . . have been . . what you . . started by asking."

"It was, and His Lordship did not argue."

"It . . cannot be . . true!" Nikola said again.

"It is!" Jimmy assured her. "And now I can do everything I want in the house, and you shall have the new stove in the kitchen you have been fussing about for so long."

"That will be . . wonderful!" Nikola cried. "You are . . quite . . certain he was not . . suspicious?"

"Why should he be?" Jimmy asked.

"It seems strange that he should have agreed to pay what you asked without haggling over it."

"We certainly "haggled", as you call it, over the Daghest and now I am asking myself if I should have let it go so cheaply."

"I think you should . . go down on your knees and thank . . God for what you have . . already received,"

83

Nikola replied, "and, Jimmy . . l have . . something to . . ask you."

"What is it?" Jimmy asked in an uncompromising voice.

"Surely . . now that you . . have so much . . this is something you need . . never do again?"

Jimmy got off the bed.

"Shall we say, not for a long time!" he replied.

"I would be happier if you said 'Never'!"

"How can I foresee what will happen in the future?" he asked.

He walked towards the communicating-door.

Nikola knew that he was irritated by her insistence.

As he reached it he said:

"If you want the truth, I am very, very pleased with myself! I think, although you may not say so, that I have been b:illiantly clever!"

He did not wait for Nikola to reply.

He went into the Boudoir and shut the door behind him.

Slowly she turned to blow out the candle by her bed.

Then as she lay down she was praying to *The Virgin in the Rose Garden*.

She was giving thanks that the danger she had feared was past.

She could still feel as if there was a stone in her breast.

. . . .

The next morning the sun was shining.

Nikola told herself the fears of the night were over.

The maid who called her said that His Lordship was going riding after breakfast.

Any of his guests who wished to go with him were welcome to do so.

Because Jimmy had praised the Marquis's horses, Nikola had hoped she might have a chance of riding.

She had therefore packed her habit.

It was an old one, but it was well cut because it had belonged to her mother.

Nikola had worn it after she had grown out of her own.

Her mother's jacket, because she hunted, was plainly tailored and fitted Nikola as if it had been made for her.

The stock she wore round her neck was rather frayed.

But she had washed and starched it since the last time she had worn it.

She managed to tie it so that it did not show where it was worn.

She had brought a hat which was not the top-hat worn in the hunting-field.

Nor was it the bowler which had been introduced a few years before.

It was a high-crowned, very attractive hat with a gauze veil.

It was worn, although Nikola was not aware of it, by the 'Pretty Horse-breakers' in London.

They were the women who broke in the horses of the Livery Stables.

Brilliant riders and extremely attractive, they were sought after by the rich "Men-About-Town".

Nikola, however, was not worrying about her appearance as she hurried downstairs.

She entered the Breakfast Room to find three men, including her brother, were there before her.

There was no sign of Lady Cleveland or of Lady Sarah.

The Marquis came in just as she was sitting down beside Jimmy.

"Good-morning!" he said to his guests.

Then he turned to Nikola and asked:

"Are you feeling better?"

"Yes . . thank you," Nikola replied.

"We missed you last night," Willie said, "but your brother managed to empty my pockets."

Nikola heaved a sigh of relief that Jimmy had not lost.

Then she remembered how much he had gained from the Marquis.

"It must have been his . . lucky night!" she said lightly.

"And we are lucky to have you with us this morning," William said gallantly. "I only hope Blake's horse will not prove too much for you!"

"I should find it very humiliating if it did," Nikola replied.

She found, however, that she was given a perfectly trained and magnificent-looking horse that was easy to handle.

Jimmy had a far more spirited one, which delighted him.

The Marquis was breaking in a stallion that did everything in its power to unseat him.

It was the age-old battle between man and beast.

Nikola thought that no man could look more magnificent or ride more brilliantly.

The Marquis took them to his race-course.

The four men raced each other while Nikola watched them.

The Marquis was the undisputed winner, and Jimmy was second.

As they rode back towards the house the Marquis asked him:

"Are you as knowledgeable about horses as you are about pictures?"

"I would like to think so," Jimmy replied, "but I do not often have the good luck to ride an animal as fine as this!"

He patted the horse he was riding as he spoke.

Nikola wondered if some of the money he had obtained might be spent on new horses for King's Keep.

The two they had were used both for drawing the Curricle and for riding.

They were not in the same class as those owned by the Marquis.

"If we could have just one really good stallion which I could ride when Jimmy is not there," she thought to herself.

Then she started when the Marquis, who must have read her thoughts said:

"I have a feeling, Miss Tancombe, that you are feeling envious."

"Of course I am!" Nikola replied. "You have so much, and we have so little."

"But you have King's Keep!" he said as if he must argue the point.

"Which is a very demanding possession," Nikola replied.

She spoke without thinking.

There was a note in her voice which made the Marquis suddenly aware that she had suffered.

Perhaps she too had made sacrifices for the house which meant so much to her brother.

He was used to being clairvoyant about people, especially when he was "on a mission".

But he had never felt it so acutely before with a woman as he did now with Nikola.

As the Marquis looked at her he thought she was very different from most women.

It was because she was so completely unselfconscious about her beauty.

She was quite unaware of how lovely she looked with her fair hair thrown into prominence by the darkness of her habit.

Also by the black horse she was riding.

Any other woman of his acquaintance after they had been galloping would be smoothing their hair and pulling their habit into place.

They would also be flirting with him with every word they spoke and with every look they gave him.

But Nikola was looking at the house that lay ahead of them.

She was also looking at the lake beneath it and the flowers that grew all around them.

It struck him that her expression was very like that of *The Virgin in the Rose Garden*.

"If an Artist saw her, he would want to paint her in a garden too," he thought, "and of course she is a virgin."

It was a strange thought for him to have.

Then as they rode on, he found himself wondering why Nikola had been frightened the night before.

Why had she left the Study with the excuse of going to bed?

Why had she been praying to *The Virgin in the Rose Garden* as soon as her brother had turned it round?

This was something he had only just thought of, and he was determined to know the answer.

CHAPTER FIVE

When they returned to the Castle the Marquis went to his Study.

He knew his Secretary would have a large number of letters waiting for him to sign.

He had just finished a dozen of them when Mr. Gordon came in and the Marquis said:

"I was just wondering, Gordon, where I have heard the name of Jacqueline de Bourgogne."

Mr. Gordon looked puzzled.

The Marquis was thinking it was very strange when Sir James Tancombe had shown him a picture by Mabuse he had known who it was.

There was silence. Then the Marquis said:

"A picture in which she is portrayed was painted by Mabuse."

"Ah! Now I think I remember, My Lord,"

Gordon replied. "It was mentioned in His late Lordship's correspondence."

"Fetch it," the Marquis ordered.

After his father died he had had his very considerable correspondence with other Collectors filed.

It was just in case he wished for details of his purchases at any time.

The name now came to his mind as it was connected with Mabuse.

Perhaps his father had received some information about it which he had read in his letters.

He went on signing his letter.

Only a few minutes passed before Mr. Gordon returned with a large file in his hand.

He put it down in front of the Marquis saying:

"This file, My Lord, contains all the correspondence regarding artists from 'L' to 'M'"

"Thank you."

The Marquis opened the file and turning over the pages found under '*MABUSE*' a letter from Lord Hartley to his father.

He had written:

"You said to me when we were in White's Club that you were anxious to acquire a Mabuse for your Collection.

I told you that I have his portrait of Jacqueline de Bourgogne. I bought it from a Dealer in Amsterdam whose name and address I have put on a separate sheet.

I think you will find him quite a reliable man, and trustworthy. It was in fact this Dealer who was instrumental in my acquiring Lochner's 'The Virgin in the Rose Garden', which is one of the most beautiful pictures I have ever seen.

It would be a great pleasure to show them to you if you ever have time to visit my house."

The Marquis stared at what had been written.

Then he saw at the end of the letter some words in his father's somewhat scribbled handwriting.

It was so badly written that he had to turn the letter towards the window to read it.

It said:

"After Hartley's death got in touch with his widow. She refused to sell anything!"

90

The Marquis put the file down on his desk and said to his Secretary:

"Ask Sir James Tancombe and his sister to come here."

Mr. Gordon hurried away to obey his orders.

The Marquis read the letter again, and also his father's note.

A little time elapsed before Jimmy and Nikola appeared.

As they came into the Study, the Marquis was aware that Nikola was again looking frightened.

He rose perfunctorily, then said:

"Will you sit down? I have something to discuss with you." Jimmy took a chair nearest to the desk.

Nikola moved to another one which was opposite the three pictures which had been arranged on the sofa.

'The Virgin in the Rose Garden' was in the centre.

As she looked at it she had the frightening feeling that it was warning her.

"When I awoke this morning," the Marquis began, "I was wondering how it was that when you showed me the portrait painted by Mabuse I knew it was of Jacqueline de Bourgogne."

Jimmy was listening with his eyes on the Marquis's face, but Nikola was looking at the picture of the Virgin.

It struck the Marquis that once again she was praying.

"I therefore," he went on, "turned up my father's files and found that he had corresponded with Lord Hartley about this very picture."

Jimmy stiffened.

Nikola felt as if she had been stabbed by a dagger.

For a moment it was impossible to breathe.

Very slowly she turned to look at the Marquis.

"I have a letter here which Lord Hartley wrote to my father," the Marquis went on, "and I will read it to you."

He picked up the file and in his clear, deep voice read the letter aloud.

When he mentioned *The Virgin in the Rose Garden* Nikola gave a little gasp.

Clasping her hands together she turned once again to look at the picture.

"Help us . . help us!" she was saying in her heart.

The Marquis finished the letter from Lord Hartley.

Then he read the note his father had made at the bottom of it.

He put the file down on his desk, and looking at Jimmy said:

"Perhaps your explanation, Sir James, is that Lady Hartley changed her mind and sold you both these pictures and the Van Leyden which I have not yet had time to check."

There was a little pause.

Then as Nikola knew that Jimmy was going to try and bluff it out she rose to her feet.

She walked to the desk to stand in front of the Marquis and said:

"Please . . please understand that . . the pictures were . . shut up in a dusty room . . and our Aunt was not . . interested in . . them."

Her voice was hardly audible.

She was very pale.

Her eyes as she pleaded with the Marquis seemed to fill her whole face.

"So you stole them!" the Marquis said.

"Lady Hartley is a Tancombe," Nikola replied, "and Jimmy . . needed them so that he could . . restore the house in which the . . Tancombes have lived for . . four-hundred years."

"Nevertheless," the Marquis said in a hard voice, "they were not your brother's to sell, and I imagine that Lady Hartley would not have given them to him had he asked her to do so."

"She would not . . help us even though . . she is very

rich," Nikola answered. "Please . . try to . . under-stand."

"I think your brother should speak for himself," the Marquis said.

Almost as if he had struck at her, Nikola moved away from the desk.

She stood in front of the picture of *The Virgin in the Rose Garden*.

Now she was praying with all her heart that the Marquis would not denounce Jimmy publicly.

"Well?" the Marquis demanded looking at Jimmy.

"Have you nothing to say for yourself?

"My sister has told you the truth," he answered. "I was desperate to restore King's Keep to its former glory and, unless the house was to fall to the ground and we were to starve, I had to obtain money from somewhere."

Jimmy spoke defiantly, and Nikola knew he was fighting for his very life.

There was silence.

Then the Marquis said:

"There are several things I can do about this."

As Jimmy did not ask the obvious question he went on:

"I can of course, send you to Lady Hartley to restore the pictures to her late husband's Collection."

"If you do that, they will just rot in the dust as they were doing before I cleaned them," Jimmy replied, "and no one will see them except the mice."

The Marquis's lips tightened a little cynically as if he thought Jimmy was putting up a good defence for his actions.

Then he continued:

"On the other hand, I can accept the pictures in good faith. In which case, I shall expect you to make reparation for attempting to deceive me."

Without looking round Nikola knew that Jimmy squared his shoulders.

93

"What do you want me to do?" he asked.

"I realise you have a great knowledge and appreciation of Art."

He paused a moment then went on:

"So in return for my keeping silent about what is unquestionably a criminal offence, I require you to do me service!"

"In what way?" Jimmy asked.

It flashed through Nikola's mind that the Marquis intended to humiliate Jimmy. She knew in that case he would never agree.

If he refused, then the Marquis might tell Lady Hartley what he had done.

If that happened, she was quite certain the story would be passed round all their relations.

That would mean that Jimmy would be ostracised and decried by every one of them.

Once the story was known to the rest of the family she was quite certain they would talk and talk.

Sooner or later it would be known by a great number of other people as well.

Because the name of Tancombe was besmirched, it would also affect King's Keep.

"That must . . not happen . . it must not!" she cried silently.

"I have had in mind for some time," the Marquis was saying, "to visit Lima, which as you know, is in Peru."

He paused, aware of the bewilderment at what he had just said on the faces of the two people listening to him.

Both Jimmy and Nikola were wondering what this had to do with them.

"And then from Lima," the Marquis went on, "To travel to Cuzco which is thousands of feet up in the mountains."

He stopped speaking for a moment, and then continued:

94

"It is where, if you remember your history, the Spaniards destroyed 363 Temples built by the Incas, and built in their place 365 Churches."

What he was saying was so surprising that Nikola turned to stare at the Marquis as her brother was doing.

"The Jesuits," the Marquis went on, "had in the 17th century, a School of Painting and their pictures are still hanging in the Churches they built."

He paused, and as they did not speak, he went on:

"Some of these, I understand are for sale, and some, especially those by Basilio Santacruz, are said to be very fine."

Because she could not help it, without really thinking, Nikola moved a little nearer to the desk.

"I intended," the Marquis went on, "as I have already said, to visit Cuzco myself, but now, I think you, Tancombe, should go in my place with a friend of mine, who is extremely shrewd when it comes to money, and knows a certain amount about pictures."

Jimmy drew in his breath.

"You mean – you want – me to buy these – pictures for you?"

"If you think they are worth buying," the Marquis replied.

"Although you will have to leave your beloved house behind, the journey should certainly enlarge your knowledge of the world and of 17th century paintings."

For a moment Jimmy was speechless.

Then he said:

"If I can really do that, then of course I can only thank Your Lordship for being extremely magnanimous and broad-minded."

"When you return," the Marquis said as if he had no wish to be thanked, "we can again discuss the payment for these three pictures, which will be safe in my keeping until then."

Because Nikola was so relieved and knew that her prayers had been answered, her eyes filled with tears.

Then as if the Marquis suddenly realised she was standing near him, he said sharply:

"I have not yet finished. Your sister, who is definitely an accessory to your crime, must also pay a price for my silence."

Nikola's eyes opened wider than they were already.

In a whisper she asked:

"W.what do you . . want me to . . do?"

"I am leaving for Greece tomorrow morning," the Marquis said. "I wish you to come with me as my companion on the journey which will include visits to the Aegean Sea in my yacht."

Nikola felt she could not have heard him aright.

It was Jimmy who said sharply:

"I would like to know, My Lord, exactly what you mean by that!"

The eyes of the two men met and the Marquis said:

"Exactly what I say. It is a long journey, and I would like to have somebody to talk to."

"And you suggest that my sister should accompany you unchaperoned?"

"It does not suit me to have a party," the Marquis said, "and as it happens, no one in England will know where I am or who is with me."

"At the same time . . .!" Jimmy began hotly.

The Marquis put up his hand.

"Your sister will be treated with all . . "

He was about to say "propriety".

Then behind Nikola he caught sight of the picture on the sofa.

" . . as if she was *The Virgin in the Rose Garden*!" he finished.

Jimmy wanted to protest that Nikola should not do anything which would jeopardise her reputation.

96

Then as if the words were forced from him against his will, he said:

"Very well, My Lord, I trust you."

"I assure you," the Marquis replied, "you will have no grounds for doing otherwise."

Nikola had no idea what they were talking about.

Looking bewildered she said:

"But of course if Your Lordship . . wants me to come with . . you I will do so . . and as James will be away it will be . . very exciting for . . me."

Jimmy pressed his lips together as if he had a great deal more to say on the matter.

Then he knew without words that the Marquis was ordering him to keep silent.

He was in fact helpless to do anything but acquiesce.

"Very well, My Lord," he said, "and when do you wish me to leave?"

"I am leaving here tomorrow morning," the Marquis replied, "and you will come with your sister and me as far as London."

He paused, then went on:

"Where the house-party is concerned, we all have appointments which cannot be cancelled."

"I understand," Jimmy said.

"I hope you do, and let me reiterate because it is important: neither you, Sir James, nor your sister is to tell anybody where you are going or with whom – do you understand? Nobody!"

His voice was harsh as he continued:

"If you do not keep silent as I have told you to do, then I shall not keep silent on a subject which concerns you!"

It was a threat which made Jimmy flush with anger.

"I promise you, My Lord," Nikola said quickly, "that we will be very careful not to do anything you do not want us to do."

Her voice was trembling as she went on:

"Thank you . . thank you for not . . denouncing Jimmy! It is . . difficult to express how truly . . grateful we are!"

She thought as she spoke that Jimmy was appearing very ungrateful.

She could not understand why he was making a fuss about her going to Greece.

Of course it was unconventional for her to go without a chaperon.

But she was sure in the circumstances that the Marquis was not going to treat her as if she were a guest, but more like a servant.

Unlike any other Lady he might have taken with him, he would give her orders.

She would have to do his bidding.

"Now we have settled that you are free to return to the house-party," the Marquis said. "But remember – not a word of anything that has been discussed here, and when we all leave together tomorrow morning, it is because you, Sir James, have a meeting in London."

Jimmy nodded as he went on:

"And I have an appointment which it is impossible for me to postpone."

"We will make no mistakes, My Lord," Jimmy said, "and I will do my very best to find you some pictures in Cuzco which will be good enough to hang in your new Gallery."

Now there was a note in his voice which told Nikola he was excited by the idea of going to a place of which she had never heard.

It was on the other side of the world.

She could hardly believe that she too was going to travel.

Anything would be better than sitting alone in King's Keep worrying about Jimmy.

She went upstairs to change out of her riding habit.

Only then did she realise she had only the few clothes she had brought with her to Ridge.

Somehow she must send home for some more.

She went through the Boudoir to James's bedroom.

She knew he would be changing.

Jimmy had changed, managing as he always did to do so without the help of a valet.

She knocked on the communicating-door and opened it.

As she went in Jimmy said before she could speak:

"I was just thinking, Nikola, that it is rather exciting going to Cuzco. I have heard about the pictures there from Papa."

He stopped speaking a moment, then went on:

"A friend of his had seen them and said they were in a bad state of repair and now that the Jesuits have all gone nobody is interested in them."

"It will be a wonderful experience for you," Nikola replied, "and I am sure it is due to my prayers that the Marquis will not tell Aunt Alice."

"Then you had better go on praying that when I come back he will give me the £10,000 he promised me!" Jimmy said.

He paused for a moment before he added:

"I suppose Butters and Bessie will look after the house all right?"

"Of course they will," Nikola replied, "and I do not suppose I shall be away for long. If nothing else, the Marquis will be back for Royal Ascot."

The worry cleared from James's eyes.

"Of course he will! I am sure he intends that his horse will win the Gold Cup."

"You had better send Butters a note and of course some money," Nikola reminded him.

"It can be taken by one of the grooms, and do you think he could bring back some of my clothes?"

Jimmy laughed.

"His Lordship, for all his planning, has not remembered that! Of course you must have clothes, whatever they look like."

"I suppose if I am to be alone on the yacht with him, they will not matter," Nikola said.

"But if his friends come aboard they may think it rather strange that I am almost in rags!"

Jimmy looked embarrassed.

"Are your things really as bad as that?"

"Worse!"

"Well, that is his business!" Jimmy remarked. "I had better go and ask him now if I can order a groom to ride as quickly as possible to King's Keep.

You must write to Bessie telling her exactly what she must pack up for you."

"If I take many clothes His Lordship will have to send a vehicle of some sort."

"Why not?" Jimmy asked as if he had just thought of it. "Heaven knows the stables are stocked with conveyances of every sort and description."

He put a finishing touch to his tie and walked towards the door.

"Leave it to me, Nikola," he said, "and I promise I will send Butters enough money to last him for at least a month."

Nikola went back to her own room.

She wondered what she should do when she returned to King's Keep if there was no money in the Bank.

Then she told herself there must be some from what Jimmy had obtained for the other things he had sold.

She only hoped the Marquis would never find out about that!

．　．　．　．　．　．　．

While brother and sister were worrying over their private affairs the Marquis was thinking of his.

It was only while he was dealing with Jimmy by sending him to Cuzco that he had remembered his own problem.

He had from the start felt nervous about taking Lady Sarah with him on his mission because she gossiped.

Last night there had arisen another reason for not taking her.

His guests had retired to bed.

Lady Cleveland said she was tired and so was her husband.

The Marquis instead of going to his bedroom had gone to his Study.

He had placed the three pictures on the sofa, as Nikola found them.

He thought as he looked again at *The Virgin in the Rose Garden* that it was one of the most attractive pictures he had ever seen.

There was no obvious resemblance to Nikola.

Yet he found himself thinking of her.

It was as if she was seated on the throne surrounded by small winged angels, her hair haloed by the sunshine.

When finally he went up to bed he decided that, although he knew Lady Sarah was waiting for him, he was not in the mood for making love to her.

It was only too obvious that was what she expected.

He knew by the way she pressed his hand when they said goodnight that she would be waiting for him to join her.

All during the evening there had been an invitation in her eyes on her lips and in every movement of her body.

It was all a repetition of what he knew only too well was the prelude to the beginning of yet another fiery affair.

"I will think about it tomorrow," he told himself as he undressed.

As his Valet carried away his evening-clothes he got into bed.

He did not blow out the candles.

He usually read for a little while before he went to sleep.

Tonight the book by his bedside which was a somewhat heavy volume on Oriental antiquities, remained unopened.

Instead he found himself thinking of the three pictures he had just acquired.

He was planning where he should hang them in his new Gallery.

He had the feeling that *The Virgin in the Rose Garden* should have a special background.

He was wondering if he should not have it in his bedroom when, to his surprise, the door opened.

It was Lady Sarah.

She was looking very lovely in a negligee that was as transparent as the nightgown she wore beneath it.

It was a deep pink, which was to be expected with her long dark hair falling over her shoulders.

She was beautiful.

Any man would have found her irresistibly desirable.

But for the moment, because she was such a contrast to *The Virgin in the Rose Garden* the Marquis felt cold.

He was in fact, only conscious of a sense of annoyance.

She had broken all the rules in visiting him rather than waiting for him to come to her.

"You have not said goodnight to me," Lady Sarah said in a soft seductive voice.

"I thought you would be too tired," the Marquis excused himself.

"How could I be that, when I was longing for you?" she answered.

She had not moved since she entered the room.

Now she sat down on the bed and very slowly put out her arms to encircle his neck.

"Why should we waste time in waiting for each other?" she whispered and her lips were on his.

. . . .

It was very much later when Lady Sarah left.

She kissed the Marquis passionately before she did so.

The Marquis knew then that even if the Prime Minister begged him to do so, he would not take Lady Sarah with him to Greece.

The difficulty was that if he did not, he would be forced to find somebody in Athens.

He did in fact, have a number of friends who were Greek.

He was sure there would be one beautiful woman amongst them who would be delighted to go with him on a cruise.

But that meant taking on board her husband also and perhaps several other guests.

It annoyed him that he had not been given more time in which to make suitable arrangements.

Yet he knew only too well that when Lord Beaconsfield required something, he wanted it "yesterday".

"Of course I will find somebody," he said doubtfully.

He was, however, absolutely determined that he would not take Lady Sarah.

Now he had decided it would be Nikola, and he congratulated himself on having been very clever.

She was young and she was innocent.

She would therefore make no demands upon him.

She was completely ignorant of the Social World.

There was no reason why their names should ever be linked in any way.

"It all fits so neatly, like a pattern," he thought "that it must be Fate."

He had been trying to visit Cuzco for over a year.

Ever since, in fact, he had learned about the pictures that were falling out of their frames and in which no one was interested.

103

Then a month ago he had decided to send a man who had bought him some pictures in Vienna.

He was delighted at the idea of the journey to Lima.

At the same time, the Marquis was sure he did not have the "flair" or the instinct which he sensed in James Tancombe.

The two of them combined would make an excellent team.

What they bought would certainly enrich his Gallery.

He was feeling in a very good humour when James came back into the Study.

"What can I do for you, Tancombe?" the Marquis asked.

Jimmy explained that he wished to send to King's Keep for Nikola's clothes.

"I also," he said, "have to instruct the servants to look after the house while I am away."

The Marquis agreed to everything.

"Should there be any difficulties before you return," he said, "I will tell your sister to notify me, and I will send over one of my staff to sort it out."

"That is very kind of you," Jimmy said, "and I suppose Nikola will be back from Greece quite quickly?"

"I sincerely hope so," the Marquis said. "It is extremely inconvenient for me to be away for long."

He paused before he added:

"As it is, I have two horses running at Newmarket next Saturday, and I would have liked to see their performance."

"There are always difficulties when one has to go away," Jimmy remarked.

"That is true," the Marquis agreed.

They walked together back to the room where the house-party had assembled before luncheon.

Nikola was already there.

As Jimmy joined her she gave him a note which he saw was addressed to Bessie.

Taking it Jimmy went from the room to the Secretary's office.

He knew that before they sat down to luncheon that a fast vehicle would have left for King's Keep.

It would be back in the evening soon after they had finished dinner.

. . . .

To Nikola travelling with the Marquis was like stepping into a Fairy Story.

They left Ridge at eight o'clock the next morning before there was any sign of Lady Cleveland or Lady Sarah.

Both Lord Cleveland and Willie, however, came to see them off.

The Marquis begged them to stay until Monday, if it suited them.

He deeply regretted that he had to leave so early.

"Sir James is in the same predicament," he said. "He has somebody of importance to see who will be leaving London tomorrow and therefore they must meet today."

"I will bet the subject they discuss is pictures!" Willie remarked.

"Could it be anything else?" Lord Cleveland asked.

The Marquis picked up the reins.

Nikola waved to the two men until the house was out of sight.

When they left the Halt in the Marquis's private train, Nikola was sure she was dreaming.

There were stewards wearing his livery to wait on them.

While she was not hungry, having recently eaten a substantial breakfast upstairs, Jimmy accepted a glass of champagne.

Later they ate Caviare and paté sandwiches.

105

Nikola knew her brother was accepting everything on the principle that he might never be offered it again.

Most certainly he could not afford it if he was paying.

When they reached Ridge House in Park Lane, the man who was going with Jimmy to Lima was waiting there.

To Nikola's relief they appeared to get on well.

The Marquis left them while he discussed his trip with Mr. Grey.

An hour after their arrival Nikola had said goodbye to Jimmy.

She was travelling alone with the Marquis to Tilbury.

A cabin on the cross-Channel Steamer to Ostend was at the Marquis's disposal.

As it was a bright sunny day, however, he preferred to walk round the deck.

Nikola read the newspapers and magazines seated comfortably in an armchair.

When they stepped ashore at Ostend she saw the Royal Railway Carriages waiting for them.

It was then that she was unable to contain her excitement.

"Is it . . really true that these belong to . . The Queen?" she asked.

"Her Majesty has most graciously put them at my disposal," the Marquis replied.

Nikola looked around her as if she could not believe her eyes.

The walls of the Drawing-Room were hung with silk *capitonnée*.

There was blue for the dado and pearl grey above, brocaded in pale yellow, with the shamrock, rose and thistle.

Four lights were set into the padded ceiling, while the curtains were blue and white.

An Indian carpet covered the floor.

There was a sofa, two armchairs in blue in Louis XVI style.

The footstool had yellow fringes and tassels.

The Sleeping-car consisted of two bedrooms.

The motif in Nikola's was Japanese with protective bamboo hung round the walls.

Dark red morocco leather covered the wash-stand and the basin.

There was plenty of room for hanging clothes.

When the train started off she went back into the Drawing-Room.

"This is very, very thrilling for me," she said to the Marquis. "In fact, I am quite sure I am dreaming!"

"As we have a long way to go," the Marquis said. "I am afraid you will find it boring before we eventually reach Greece."

Nikola smiled.

"I noticed when we came aboard that there was a large case marked '*BOOKS*'."

"So you are an avid reader?" the Marquis remarked.

"It is only in books that I have travelled so far," Nikola replied, "but I have visited a great number of countries."

Do you consider yourself knowledgeable on Greece?"

"Will there by any chance of our seeing Athens?" she asked.

"I am making no promises," the Marquis replied. "My yacht will be waiting for us, and I think it might be a mistake not to go aboard immediately."

He saw the disappointment in Nikola's eyes.

But she did not plead with him as any other woman would have done in order to get her own way.

He had established from the very beginning that if he wanted to read the newspapers he did not wish to be interrupted.

He therefore raised his newspaper until he was hidden behind it.

Then, because he was curious he looked round it to see what Nikola was doing.

She had moved from the seat opposite him to a chair by the window.

She was looking out.

She was obviously completely absorbed by the country-side through which they were passing.

She had removed her hat when she went to her bed-room.

The Marquis thought her profile silhouetted against the window was very lovely.

So was her hair, as the sunshine turned it to little tongues of fire.

Then he congratulated himself that she was keeping quiet.

That was exactly what he wanted on the journey.

When they reached Athens he would tell her what part she had to play.

That was just in case some inquisitive persons came aboard.

He doubted if it would occur to her that those who did call on him would assume she was his mistress.

"That is important," he thought. "People just have to believe that I am having a quiet holiday and that includes both the Russians and the Turks"

Then he told himself it was too soon to start worrying about what would happen.

It could wait until they were at sea.

He returned to reading the newspaper.

. . . .

When it was time for dinner, Nikola wondered what she should wear.

She had told Bessie to send her everything she thought she would need.

But she still had only one decent evening-gown.

She was quite certain that the Marquis would change into his evening-clothes.

"How could he do anything else," she asked herself with a smile, "considering we are at the moment Royalty?"

It was thrilling to think she was sleeping in the Queen's own bed.

It had never struck her for a moment that there was any significance in that the Marquis was just along the corridor.

Dawkins was accommodated in the Day Car.

There was a compartment used by the Queen's Scottish servant who always travelled with her.

In the Sleeping Car which was connected by a short corridor there were only the two bedrooms and a compartment for light luggage.

Dawkins told Nikola that the maids slept on sofas.

"Then it is fortunate we do not have any with us," Nikola laughed, "as they must be uncomfortable."

"Oi'll look after yer, Miss," Dawkins said, "an' don't yer forget t'ask fer anythin' you needs."

"Thank you," Nikola replied, thinking he was a kind little man.

He had unpacked her luggage for her.

Now she looked in the large built-in cupboard which served as a wardrobe.

She thought how shabby everything looked.

Except for her new turquoise gown.

"I can hardly wear that every night," she thought. "And anyway, I do not suppose the Marquis will notice me.'

She put on a white muslin gown she had made herself.

She had not been able to afford enough material to make a bustle.

Instead she wore a sash she had as a child, which made a large bow at the back.

109

To make it more fashionable she had added a long muslin flounce at each end.

She looked at herself in the mirror.

It did not compare with the very smart gowns which Lady Sarah had worn.

She could not help wondering why the Marquis had not asked Lady Sarah to accompany him on this trip.

She would have looked very decorative and very beautiful in the Royal Drawing-Room.

Nikola did the best she could with her hair.

She tried to achieve a fashionable coiffure.

But little curls would keep escaping.

Finally she gave up trying to brush them straight.

Without looking any more at her reflection she went into the Drawing-Room.

The Marquis looked at her, she thought, critically as she sat down opposite him.

A steward offered her a glass of champagne.

Remembering what Jimmy had said, she accepted it.

The Marquis, she thought, was looking magnificent.

He looked exactly as if he was going to dine with The Queen.

His shirt looked dazzlingly white with just one stud in the centre.

It consisted of a large black pearl.

Nikola had never seen a black pearl before.

She kept glancing at it curiously.

"What has happened to your beautiful turquoise gown which matched my Drawing-Room at Ridge?" the Marquis asked.

There was a little pause before Nikola said:

"As it is the . . only nice gown I have . . I thought I would . . keep it for some . . special occasion."

"And you do not consider that dining with me is one?"

"Yes . . of course . . it is!" Nikola replied blushing.

"But as you . . saw it last night . . and the night before . .
I thought my appearance might become . . somewhat
monotonous."

"It is certainly a very beautiful gown!" the Marquis
remarked.

Nikola laughed.

"Why are you laughing?" he asked.

"Because it is really a pair of bed-curtains!"

The Marquis stared at her.

"I do not understand what you are saying."

"When you invited my brother to stay with you . . I
had only a day and a half in which to . . make myself
something . . decent to wear."

"You made it yourself?" the Marquis asked in astonishment.

"I took the curtains from the four-poster on which
Mama had hung them."

"I see you are a very talented young woman!" the
Marquis remarked.

He did not make it sound particularly a compliment.

Nikola said apologetically:

"I am afraid you are going to be very . . ashamed
of . . me if we meet any of . . your friends. But if it
is in the evening . . then I can . . wear the turquoise
gown."

"And if it is in the day-time?" the Marquis enquired.

Nikola made a helpless little gesture with her hands.

"Then you will just have to explain that you have rescued me from a desert island where I have been stranded
for months, and I lost everything I possessed in a storm
at sea."

The Marquis laughed.

"I see you have a very active imagination, Miss
Tancombe."

He paused, then he added:

"No, that is wrong. If we are going on this long journey

together I must certainly call you 'Nikola', which I think is a very attractive name."

"My mother chose it. There are in fact, a number of Tancombes who have lived at King's Keep and were called Nikola, otherwise I would have been christened something different."

"Does your whole life revolve around that house?" the Marquis asked.

"Of course!" Nikola replied. "We have nothing else of any importance, and therefore everything is judged by whether King's Keep does or does not approve of it!"

The way she spoke made the Marquis laugh.

Then he said:

"You are certainly very different from what I expected!"

"What . . did you expect?"

"To answer that question might sound rude," he said. "Instead, I shall find it very interesting to discover how different you are."

"Then do not do it too quickly," Nikola begged. "Otherwise you will be so bored by the time we reach Athens that you may send me back in an . . ordinary train."

The Marquis was laughing again.

When he went to bed it seemed to him that they had laughed a great deal at dinner.

Nikola had an amusing way of saying things.

He could only describe by the same word "different".

He was used to dining with women who flirted with him from the first to the last course.

Their conversation had a *double entendre* in everything they said.

Nikola did not try to be witty.

But he realised that she had thought intelligently about every subject they discussed.

She had an original way of describing things which he found intriguing.

112

When he asked her if, as she had said at Ridge, her aunt, Lady Hartley, was mean to them, Nikola replied:

"When Aunt Alice dies, she will be the richest person in the graveyard."

Later as the Marquis got into a comfortable bed he thought how fortunate he was not to be travelling with Lady Sarah.

It would have meant all the conversation would have been about Love.

In some form or another it would have lasted from the time they left Ostend until the time they returned.

He had known after he had made love to her on Friday night that he was no longer attracted by her.

Her undeniable dark beauty did not now even arouse his admiration.

The next morning she had behaved in a very possessive manner which he had found embarrassing.

He was furious at the expression in both Lord Cleveland's and Willie's eyes.

He knew they were aware of what had taken place the previous night.

When he had gone up to bed on Saturday night the Marquis's mouth was set in a hard line.

He told himself he would be damned if he would be seduced unwillingly by any woman, whoever she might be.

He had therefore done something he had never done before in the whole of his life.

He had left his own bedroom and spent the night in the Guest-Room on the other side of it.

If Sarah had visited him, as he suspected she would when he did not go to her, he was not aware of it.

He had left the next morning before she could look at him reproachfully.

Now he thought with relief, he was free for at least a short time from all designing women.

Nikola was young and innocent.

She was also too unsophisticated to have any idea of how to pursue a man.

She was therefore, he told himself, exactly what he had asked for a companion.

She would assist him without being aware of it in carrying out the Prime Minister's instructions.

CHAPTER SIX

"Checkmate! I have won!" Nikola cried. "I have won! I have won!"

The Marquis looked somewhat ruefully at the chessboard.

"I must have been asleep," he said.

"Now you are being mean," she retorted. "It has taken me a long time, but at last I have beaten you."

She was so delighted that the Marquis once again found himself laughing.

He had thought it extraordinary that she had made him laugh so much in the train.

Yet since leaving Athens he had been laughing all the way up the Aegean Sea.

It was not that Nikola said anything witty.

Not in the way Lady Sarah or the other sophisticated women he knew would have spoken.

It was simply that she was so young and enthusiastic about everything.

He had learnt while they were still in the train how she spent so much time alone.

It had made her think and reason things out for herself.

It was therefore very exciting for her to be able, for the first time in her life, to air her views.

Although she did not say so, it was something new to be listened to.

Her father had talked to her exclusively about his pictures.

That included talking about various people who had better collections than his own.

Her mother had loved her.

In conversations with Nikola she had tried to make her a sweet, gentle, compassionate woman, which was what her own mother had been.

With Jimmy it was quite hopeless.

Jimmy breathed thought and lived only for King's Keep.

Now, to Nikola's delight, she found herself with a man who was extremely clever and widely travelled.

Because there was no one else, he had to talk to her.

At the same time she was very afraid of boring him.

She tentatively suggested to Dawkins that his Master might play Chess.

She discovered to her delight that the Marquis was considered an outstanding player in his Club.

Nikola had been taught how to play Chess by her father.

They wiled away the long winter evenings at King's Keep.

They would play as the wind whistled outside the windows and there was nothing left to say about the pictures.

Sir Arthur had also taught his daughter at a very early age how to play Backgammon.

It was Dawkins who had prudently brought in the Marquis's luggage both a Chess and a Backgammon board.

"How can you have been so clever as to think of them!" she exclaimed.

Dawkins had grinned.

"Oi knows wot 'is Lordship's like when 'e's bored," he said, "an' I can tell you this, Miss – 'e bores easy!"

Nikola was worried in case she bored him so much that he sent her home alone.

She was so humble about herself that she had no idea that the Marquis found himself surprisingly intrigued by her.

She was so different from what he had expected.

At the same time he was impatient to return to England.

He therefore did not stop in Athens or contact any of his friends there.

Instead he had hurried Nikola from the train down to the harbour.

The Sea Horse was waiting for him there.

The Marquis had found his yacht useful on several missions he had undertaken on behalf of the Foreign Office.

He had therefore installed larger and more powerful engines than any other private vessel afloat.

Nikola was not aware of this.

All she knew was that it was the most splendid yacht she could imagine.

She soon learnt it had the smartest crew, combined with an almost unbelievable comfort and luxury.

The Marquis's Chef was a Frenchman.

This meant Nikola told him, that the food might have come from Mount Olympus.

"In fact," she added, "as it was taken aboard at Athens, it obviously did!"

She felt a little wistfully that she would have liked to see the Acropolis.

She could not understand why the Marquis should be in such a hurry to put to sea.

He thought it was a mistake to make explanations which might make her curious.

Privately he had told the Captain to make all possible speed towards Constantinople.

He had only made one concession in Athens.

It was to send Dawkins, the very instant the train arrived, to buy every newspaper obtainable, regardless of the language in which it was printed.

117

Dawkins had arrived at *The Sea Horse* only five or ten minutes after the Marquis and Nikola.

He had bought the most extraordinary collection of newspapers.

Those printed in the different languages of the Balkans were several days old.

But they told the Marquis what was happening in the war between Russia and Turkey.

He learnt that the Russians had moved even nearer to Constantinople.

It made him think that if any protests were to come from England they might be too late.

If he was to carry out the Prime Minister's instructions it was extremely important that he find out what exactly the Russians intended.

He had been very careful what he said on the train.

He had no wish to make Nikola inquisitive.

He thought she might ask why he had left England so quickly.

He wondered how he would answer her should she question his purpose in visiting Constantinople at this particular moment.

Then he remembered she was English.

She would know little or nothing about what was happening in the East.

He was therefore astonished when she remarked casually:

"Count Ignatiev, the Tsar's emissary, has with his new Treaty with Turkey proposed a swollen Bulgaria to stretch from the Black Sea to the Aegean."

For a moment the Marquis could not believe what he had heard.

Then he asked sharply:

"Who told you that:"

"I was reading about it in one of the newspapers," Nikola replied. "It stated that virtually the whole of the Balkans is now under Russian control."

"Show me the newspaper," the Marquis ordered.

The newspapers had all been piled on top of a table in the Saloon.

Nikola turned them over until she found the one she wanted.

She handed it to the Marquis who stared at it before he said:

"But this is Greek! Are you telling me that you speak Greek?"

"Not very well," Nikola admitted, "and Papa said my accent was lamentable! But I find it quite easy to read."

"You surprise me!" the Marquis said dryly.

He read the article in the newspaper which Nikola pointed out to him.

He was aware that the Greeks were extremely apprehensive at the Russian invasion of countries so near to them.

He thought however, it would be a mistake to discuss it with Nikola.

He threw the newspaper down and challenged her to a game of Backgammon.

Now the weather was warm.

Nikola wore a thin gown which Bessie had packed for her.

While the Marquis said nothing he realised how worn and shabby it was.

It was Dawkins who said to him in the privacy of his cabin:

"A nicer young lady's never come aboard wi' us, M'Lord!"

The Marquis made no comment and Dawkins went on:

"If yer asks me, it's a cryin' shame 'er clothes be so thread bare. A beggar wouldn't give a 'thank ye' for 'em!"

"I am aware of that," the Marquis replied briefly.

He knew by the way Dawkins looked at him that he was thinking he might have done something about it.

But he knew perceptively that if he had offered Nikola some new gowns, she would have refused.

She was quite unperturbed by them herself.

The Marquis was sure that her mother had instilled in her a very strict sense of propriety.

Carelessly, when speaking of Lady Lessington, whose photograph Nikola had seen in one of the magazines she was reading in the train, he had said cynically:

"She glitters like a diamond, and it is a stone for which she has an insatiable desire."

"Then Lord Lessington must be very rich," Nikola remarked innocently.

The Marquis thought of the extremely expensive necklace he had given Lady Lessington before they parted.

He wondered what Nikola would say if he offered to buy her some jewels.

Then he knew she would be shocked and bewildered by such a suggestion.

She had no idea that Ladies in the Social World would accept any present that was more expensive than a bottle of scent – or perhaps a fan.

Last night after they had dined together, the stars had shone brilliantly overhead.

He had found himself wondering what colour, apart from the turquoise blue of her best gown, would suit Nikola.

He thought it would be amusing to choose her clothes.

He had chosen those of several pretty Ballerinas.

He had also done the same for several of his Social loves to give them an appropriate frame for their beauty.

Nikola had a very unusual loveliness, he thought.

She was also completely unselfconscious about it.

He was quite certain a great number of people would not realise how beautiful she was.

It was like, he thought, seeing a tree stripped of its leaves and being not as perfect as it should be.

He was still thinking of how he would dress Nikola when he was alone in the darkness of his cabin.

It was large and very luxurious.

As she was such a skilful needlewoman, he thought she could more than likely turn the satin bed-cover or the curtains over the port-hole into a gown.

The idea amused him.

Then he thought he would like to take her to Paris.

He would dress her in Parisian clothes which would be as dazzling as her eyes when they lit up with laughter.

Then he told himself he had something more important to think about.

Nikola was just a girl he had brought with him merely as a companion.

Even so, he found himself before he went to sleep thinking of her in a garden of roses.

There were winged angels peeping at her through the flowers.

. . . .

To Nikola, every day was more exciting than the last.

By this time, she was sure that the Marquis had some very important reason for his journey.

Because he obviously did not wish to speak of it, she kept her thoughts to herself.

At the same time she was extremely curious.

Jimmy had spoken of the Marquis as being a great sportsman and a famous Collector of pictures.

He had never hinted at any Political interests or activities.

Yet now Nikola guessed the reason for the Marquis travelling at such speed.

It had something to do with the war between Russia and Turkey.

England was not involved.

But people like the Prime Minister, and perhaps the Queen must be concerned at the way Russia was taking over so much of Europe.

They had, to all intents and purposes, annexed the Balkans.

Now they had turned their attention to Turkey.

As she thought about it, she remembered Natasha's father saying that the Russians always talked about Constantinople as their rightful Capital City.

That was what they were fighting for.

If the Russians acquired it, it would, she thought, unbalance the power in Europe.

As they reached the Sea of Marmara it was growing late in the evening.

They anchored in a bay on the North shore.

"I think we should turn in early," the Marquis said soon after dinner.

Nikola gave him a quick glance.

She realised, although he was hiding it from her, that he had a reason for such a suggestion.

They had walked from the Saloon out on deck.

She saw in the light from the moon which was high in the sky that they were in a small bay.

Behind a sandy beach were some low cliffs that appeared easy to climb.

The Marquis was looking at them at the same time as she was.

There was a rough path leading from the bay itself onto the ground above it.

Everything was very silent.

Nikola had expected to hear the distant roar of guns or at least some sign of war.

As the Marquis was obviously waiting for an answer to his remark she replied:

"Yes, of course we should turn in. Do you think we will reach Constantinople tomorrow:"

"I have not decided yet whether I shall call there," he said in an enigmatic manner.

She was well aware what he meant.

It was that he had no intention of discussing the probability of it with her.

She therefore dropped him the graceful little curtsy.

It was what she always accorded him at night and said:

"Goodnight, My Lord. I hope you sleep well, and it is very exciting to have come so far so quickly."

"Goodnight, Nikola," the Marquis replied.

He waited a few minutes for her to reach her cabin and shut herself in.

Then he went to his own.

Dawkins was waiting for him.

He changed quickly from his evening-dress into plain unobtrusive clothes that might have been worn by a well-to-do Russian.

Dawkins gave him a loaded revolver and a sharp dagger-like knife.

The Marquis concealed both on his person.

"Now, don't you go takin' no chances, M'Lord!" Dawkins said. "You knows we can't trust them 'Ruskies'!"

"If my information is correct I shall be taking no risks, but merely calling on a friend."

"Oi wouldn't trust any so-called 'friends' in this part of th' world!" Dawkins remarked.

"Do not worry about me," the Marquis answered. "And if anything unexpected happens, take Miss Tancombe to the British Embassy in Athens."

"Don't you go talkin' like that, M'Lord!" Dawkins said, "an' remember – you're more use t' yer country alive than dead!"

The Marquis laughed.

It was the sort of remark that Dawkins always made on such occasions.

He hurried up the companionway.

123

A boat rowed by two seamen was waiting to take him into the sandy beach of the bay.

. . . .

Nikola heard him leave and knew that he was going ashore.

She thought it was very brave of him.

At the same time it was foolhardy.

Surely the Russians would be watching the coast in case they were attacked by the Turks:

If the information in the newspapers was correct, they had advanced even nearer to Constintinople than they had been before.

One newspaper she had read had hinted that they had reached San Stefano.

Suddenly she was frightened for the Marquis.

She began praying that he would be safe and come to no harm.

It was terrifying to think of him as a prisoner in the hands of men who would not realise his importance.

They could treat him roughly.

They might kill or imprison him.

"He is so magnificent!" she thought. "He is like his great Stallion and I could not bear to think of either of them suffering."

She was praying fervently.

Then the picture of *The Virgin in the Rose Garden* appeared before her.

She thought there was the fragrance of roses in her cabin.

She knew The Virgin was listening to her prayer.

Because the view had been so lovely when she stood on deck with the Marquis, she pulled back the curtains over her portholes.

Now shafts of moonlight flooded into her cabin, turning everything to silver.

It was so beautiful.

It seemed impossible that anything so cruel and bestial as war was happening only a short distance away.

Men were killing each other.

Just from the greed to possess more land and rule over more unfortunate and helpless people.

Perhaps in some marvellous way of his own, Nikola thought, the Marquis would help to bring about peace.

The Russians would have to be content with what they already had.

The Turks would cease torturing the Bulgarians.

As she prayed, it made her think of how helpless women were when men wished physically to assault each other.

All that was left for women to do was to pray.

She knew that if the Marquis died, she would feel that she had lost something very wonderful.

He had come quite unexpectedly into her life.

How could she believe that only a week or so ago she had been alone at King's Keep and Jimmy away?

Now she had been transplanted as if by magic into the Sea of Marmara.

There was a belligerent Russia on one side and a defiant Turkey on the other.

"Stop them . . please . . stop them," she prayed to The Virgin. "Let them find peace and, above all, do not let . . the Marquis be in any . . real danger."

Suddenly she heard footsteps running down the companionway and along the passage which led to his room.

To her astonishment, however, instead of opening the door beyond hers, he came into her cabin.

He ran towards the bed.

As he did so she saw with amazement that he was pulling off his coat, then his shirt.

She had been almost asleep, although she was praying for him.

125

Now she could only stare at him as if she was dreaming.

He kicked off his shoes, flung his clothes under the bed and pulling back the sheets got in beside her.

As he did so he spoke for the first time.

"They are just behind me!" he whispered.

Then he put his arms around her and pulled her against him.

Nikola could hardly believe it was really happening.

Before her lips could move or she could be aware of anything except the closeness of the Marquis, the door opened.

The Marquis was holding her so close that she could not see.

She was aware, however, that two men had entered the cabin.

One of them was carrying a lantern.

It lit up the cabin which was already bright with moonlight.

The Marquis had both his arms around Nikola so that her head was on his shoulder.

Her face was hidden against his neck.

For a moment he did not move.

Then he looked up and asked in a tone of astonishment.

"What the Devil are you doing here?"

His arms slackened slightly, but he still held Nikola against him.

She was conscious that the men could see his naked chest and arms.

"Pardon Excellency!" one of the men answered slowly in English with a very pronounced accent. "We see – man come aboard – this ship and . . "

"A man?" the Marquis interrupted. "Why should that concern you? If my seamen have been ashore, they were, I assure you, doing no harm."

"This not – seaman we see – Excellency," the Russian replied.

"Then look for him elsewhere," the Marquis said sharply, "and get out of this cabin!"

The Russian who had spoken came a little nearer.

Now, by turning her head very slightly Nikola could see him through her hair which was falling over her shoulders.

He was a large, commanding-looking man.

It was clear to her then that the man who had spoken was the leader.

The other who was holding the lantern was his inferior.

The one nearest to the bed had a revolver in his hand. .

She could also see the hilt of a dagger at his waist.

He was not in uniform, but wore a Russian fur hat on his head.

His dark clothes proclaimed him as a man of some importance.

"I told you to get out!" the Marquis said. "If you want any information about my men, talk to my Captain."

"Your Excellency come – ashore with – me," the Russian demanded. "There – many questions must be – asked by the – Officer in Charge of this – region."

As the Russian spoke Nikola was aware that the Marquis had stiffened.

Because he had raised himself to speak to the intruders her head was a little further down on his chest.

She could therefore hear his heart beating violently.

It was not only with breathlessness as when he had entered the cabin, but also because he was apprehensive.

She was sure there was every reason for him to be afraid.

Quite suddenly she knew what she must do.

To the Marquis's surprise she moved from the shelter of his arms.

She sat up in bed pulling the sheet up over her breasts.

Now she could see the Russian clearly.

127

She was certain he was a real danger to the Marquis.

She stared at him for a long second as she collected her thoughts.

Then she said angrily in Russian:

"How dare you come here interfering in what is my case! I was sent here by the Third Section and I take my orders from the Chief and no one else!"

She made a gesture with her hand and went on:

"This gentleman fortunately does not understand Russian, but you are making it very difficult for me and I shall report you for incompetence! Go away immediately, and apologise by saying you have made a mistake."

As she continued to speak the Russians stared at her in sheer astonishment.

She went on, her voice sharpening and growing more aggressive with every word she spoke.

Suddenly the Russian seemed to shrival and grow smaller.

"I did not know, Gracious Lady," he said, "that you were here. In fact, we had no idea."

"Does the Third Section have to explain itself to underlings?" Nikola asked furiously. "You have stumbled into something which does not concern you!"

She paused to give them an angry stare before continuing:

"What has been planned is far too important to be spoilt by an idiotic mistake made by fools who cannot see beyond their noses!"

She used words in Russian which were very rude.

Natasha had taught them to her as a joke.

The Russian to whom she was speaking crumbled.

"Forgive me – I very apologetic – I no idea you were here!"

"Of course you had no idea!" Nikola retorted. "Now stop talking and making things worse than they are already.

128

As I have already said, this is my case, and mine alone, so get out!"

The Russian bowed his head and made a sweeping gesture with his hands.

"Apologise!" Nikola ordered.

"Forgive me – Your Excellency," he said to the Marquis. "It all a mistake – we leave ship – immediately."

He did not wait for the Marquis to reply, but turned and went out of the cabin.

As he did so, Nikola, who was trembling, turned towards the Marquis.

She was suddenly very frightened.

He knew that although the Russians had left the cabin they had not closed the door.

It was the oldest trick in the world to appear to have left but to eavesdrop.

Just in case something worth hearing was said inadvertently, they would listen.

The Marquis was afraid that Nikola might speak.

To keep her silent his lips came down on hers.

For a moment she could not believe it was happening.

She had spoken on impulse and been carried away by her own words.

Only when the Russians left the cabin did she feel it was impossible that she had been successful.

That she had actually saved the Marquis from interrogation.

She knew what this could mean.

The fear of it made her almost collapse.

Then as the Marquis kissed her she did not believe it was happening.

His lips took possession of hers.

She knew it was the most perfect and wonderful thing that could possibly happen.

She had never imagined that a man so overwhelmingly omnipotent would take any interest in her as a woman.

But now, his arms were round her and his lips held her mouth captive.

As his heart beat against her she felt a sensation she had never experienced before.

It was as if the moonlight was moving through her body, into her breasts and touching her lips.

It was so wonderful, so perfect, that she thought for a moment that she must have died.

She was being carried by the angels up into Heaven.

Without meaning to, not only her lips, but also her whole being surrendered itself to the Marquis.

She felt an indescribable ecstasy.

It was the beauty she had seen, felt and heard in the flowers, the trees, the sky.

Yet it was even more wonderful, more perfect.

It was part of everything she expressed in her prayers.

She was not aware that the Marquis had kissed her to prevent her from saying anything the Russians might overhear.

Then he had felt the softness and innocence of her lips.

It became a kiss that was different from any kiss he had ever given or received before.

Vaguely at the back of his mind he heard the Russians moving away down the passage.

Yet he went on kissing Nikola.

It was then he knew that the blood was throbbing in his temples.

His whole body was vividly conscious of her.

The sensations she was arousing in him were an ecstasy that surpassed any feeling he had ever known.

He desired her with every nerve in his body and with his brain.

It was with a superhuman effort that he raised his head.

Then, as if the empty cabin brought him back to reality, he said:

130

"They have gone!"

Nikola did not answer.

She was looking at him with eyes that seemed in the moonlight to be filled with stars.

The Marquis got out of bed.

He bent down and pulled his shirt and his coat from beneath it, and also his shoes.

In a voice that did not sound like his own he said:

"I can only thank you, Nikola, for saving me from what would have been a very unpleasant experience."

"You . . you are . . quite . . certain they . . have gone?"

Nikola's voice came in little jerks from between her lips.

"They have gone!" the Marquis affirmed. "Now you must go to sleep. There will be no further dramatics – tonight at any rate!"

He went from the cabin and shut the door behind him.

"H.he . . kissed me," Nikola whispered to the moonlight, "he kissed me . . and . . I . . love . . him!"

CHAPTER SEVEN

Nikola did not feel happy until dawn came.

Until then she was listening.

She was terribly afraid that at the last moment something would go wrong and the Marquis would be taken away.

She was aware, however, that when he had left her he had sent for Dawkins.

A short while later the engines of the yacht had started up.

She heaved a sigh of relief.

Yet at the same time, it was impossible not to listen, just in case the Russians had hidden themselves aboard.

They might try to kill the Marquis while he was unaware that they were there.

She had always hated the Russians for what they had done to Natasha.

Now she knew the Marquis was embroiled with them she was terrified.

She had saved him once, but could she go on doing so?

She wanted to run into his cabin, to find out if he was there.

Then to beg him on her knees to return to England.

Why should he risk his life?

What was happening was not England's war, and therefore not his concern.

Then at last she fell asleep.

When Nikola awoke the sunshine was pouring in through the portholes.

The engines had stopped and the quietness made her jump out of bed to see where they were.

One look told her they were in the harbour in Constantinople.

She dressed quickly then ran up the companionway to the Saloon.

She found no one there except Dawkins, who said cheerily:

"'Mornin', Miss! That were a fine 'ow-do-ye-do' last night!"

Nikola realised that he knew what had happened and she asked:

"How did those . . men get aboard?"

"There were six o' them," Dawkins replied, "and our two on guard was no match for 'em."

"And . . they have . . all . . g.gone:"

The question came incoherently from between her lips.

"We've left 'em behind an' 'Is Lordship says it's all due to you!" Dawkins replied with a grin.

Nikola drew in her breath.

"Will he . . be safe? Supposing the Turks . . ?"

"'Is Lordship'll be all right," Dawkins interrupted. "'E's sent for a carriage an' an armed guard, so don't you go worryin' about 'im."

He served her breakfast while he was talking and poured her out a cup of coffee.

There were a thousand things she wanted to ask.

But she knew it would be wrong to question the Marquis's servants.

Yet because she was still so anxious, she found it impossible to eat.

After a little while she rose from the table and walked out on deck.

She looked up at the minarets and the dome of a mosque towering above the harbour.

She was praying that the Marquis was safe.

Then her love for him seemed to sweep over her like a tidal wave.

. . . .

The Marquis also had very little sleep after what might have been a horrifying experience.

He was also concerned by what he had heard when he had gone ashore.

When he reached the British Embassy, he was received immediately by the Ambassador.

He told him briefly what he had learnt, and it was confirmed by His Excellency.

The Marquis then went immediately to a well guarded room from which a cable could be sent directly to the Prime Minister.

It was now out of date since the British had laid a Submarine Cable which surfaced only at British possessions between London and Bombay.

But the one which ran across Europe to Constantinople was still in use.

The Ambassador assured him that, as far as he knew, the Russians had not tampered with it.

The Marquis therefore sent in a special secret code a cable to the Prime Minister saying:

"SITUATION DANGEROUS, UNLESS BRITAIN MAKES STRONG GESTURE OF PROTEST RUSSIANS WILL TAKE CONSTANTINOPLE. IMMEDIATE ACTION IMPERATIVE."

The Marquis knew that the Prime Minister would understand.

He could only hope that he would be able with the help of the Queen to force the Cabinet to take action.

134

He then thanked the Ambassador and returned to the yacht.

He saw Nikola waiting for him and was aware of the joy in her eyes that he was safe.

He was however deliberately casual.

He bade her good-morning and went to see the Captain.

The engines started up.

The Sea Horse began to move with incredible swiftness towards the Sea of Marmara.

The Marquis remained on the bridge until it was luncheon time.

When he joined Nikola she longed to ask him what was happening.

He must have known her feelings, but volunteered no information.

She thought it a mistake to try to force a confidence he did not wish to give.

Only when the stewards had left the Saloon did the Marquis say:

"I am interested to know how you can speak Russian, and why you did not tell me you could do so."

Nikola smiled.

"You did not ask me, and as I hate the Russians I am not proud of having learnt their language."

"Why do you hate them?" the Marquis enquired.

She told him about Natasha and the way she and her family had been sent to Siberia.

"And you friend also told you about the *Third Section*?" The Marquis asked.

He had been absolutely astonished at what Nikola had said to the Russians.

He could not have imagined in his wildest dreams that from a quiet unsophisticated English girl.

The most secret police in the world, they were answerable only to the Tzar.

Natasha told her how they were formed by Tzar Nicholas I who put his friend Count Benokendorff in charge.

The Marquis knew this was true.

"And it was they," Nikola went on, "who made the Tzar exile Natasha's father, and I suspect, told him to return to Russia and then sent him to Siberia."

"It must have upset you," the Marquis said sympathetically. "at the same time, I could not believe when I heard you dismiss those men so cleverly."

"I am sure it was . . Papa who told me . . what to do," Nikola replied. "I was very . . very afraid that if they . . took you away I would . . never see . . you again."

"Would that upset you?" the Marquis asked.

She wanted to say that, because she loved him, if he died she would want to die too.

But she knew he would find it embarrassing.

"He . . must never . . never know that . . I love him!" she told herself.

As if the Marquis did not wish to press the question they talked of other things.

Soon he left her to go back on the bridge.

It was after they had dinner together that the Marquis said briefly that he had no wish to talk.

Instead he read one of the books he had brought aboard with him.

It was then that Nikola thought miserably that he was bored with her.

The reason they were steaming so swiftly was that he was eager to return to England.

Because it was agonising to sit silent beside him in the Saloon, she went to bed early.

She was very tired, but when she fell asleep there were tears on her cheeks.

. . . .

136

The next day and the day after made Nikola feel more and more unhappy.

She was near the Marquis, she could see him.

She was aware that every time he spoke to her, her whole being leapt towards him.

But she knew he had withdrawn into himself.

She tried to find the reason.

Finally she decided it must be because he regretted having kissed her and was afraid she might take advantage of the fact.

She walked forlornly round the deck in the sunshine.

All the time she did so she was thinking of the Marquis.

She was wishing she could be beside him on the bridge.

At mealtimes their laughter seemed to have disappeared.

She had the feeling he did not want even to look at her.

"What has . . happened? What have . . I done . . wrong?" she asked.

Her brain told her that the Marquis had come on this voyage for one reason and one reason only.

It was to find out what was the situation between the Russians and the Turks.

He had gone ashore, then visited the British Embassy in Constantinople.

His mission, if that was what it was, had been completed.

Now he could go home.

She was sure he was counting the hours to when he could see Lady Sarah, or some Beauty like her, again.

"He has no further . . use for me," Nikola told herself unhappily. "I am just a . . makeshift companion, and now all he wants is to be . . rid of me as . . quickly as . . possible."

She cried into her pillow.

But she was determined not to be an encumbrance or to cling to him as Dawkins had told her a great many other women had tried to do.

"They're like clingin' ivy, that's wot they be!" he had said when he was tidying her cabin, "an' uses me, they do, if you can believe it, Miss, t' get into 'is good books!"

"How do they do that?" Nikola enquired.

She knew it was wrong to talk about the Marquis to Dawkins.

But he obviously was devoted to his Master and admired him so tremendously.

He was therefore like a protective Nanny or an ancient relation who had always loved him.

Dawkins had grinned at her question.

"Sometimes they slips a few sovereigns into me and," he answered, "an' say:

"If you'll say something nice about me to 'is Lordship, there's more where those came from!"

Dawkins laughed.

"Bribery an' corruption I calls it, but I'd be a mug if I said no!"

"And do you say something nice about them to His Lordship?" Nikola asked.

"I tells 'im wot I thinks is the truth," Dawkins answered, "an' nine times out o' ten, 'Is Lordship agrees with me!"

Nikola told herself she could never be like that.

'I would never degrade myself by bribing a servant to talk about me,' she thought proudly.

One thing was certain, that the Marquis would make up his own mind.

Nothing and nobody would change it.

"He is bored and tired of me," she told herself for the hundredth time.

She felt the tears come into her eyes.

．　．　．　．　．　．　．

The Sea Horse reached Athens in what was undoubtedly record time.

They docked at two o'clock in the morning.

It was only when Nikola woke up that she realised the rush was over.

The noise and tremor of the engines had ceased.

Now everything was very quiet and peaceful.

She knew without being told that they had reached Athens.

It was then she prayed to *The Virgin in the Rose Garden* that the Marquis would not leave as hurriedly as when they had arrived.

"Let him . . stay here for . . just a . . few days," she pleaded. "It would be so . . wonderful to be . . with him . . in Greece."

She knew she felt like that because she thought of the Marquis as a Greek God.

She wanted above all things for him to show her the Acropolis.

He would explain to her what was left of the greatness of Greece when it had altered the thinking of the world.

Then she knew that she was really not so much interested in Greece as in him.

Even to be with him in the train would be an inexpressible joy.

But she felt an agonising pain because every hour every minute took her nearer to the moment when he would say goodbye to her.

After that she would never see him again.

The sands of time were running out.

She knew that even if he was indifferent and bored with her she could at least be near him.

She jumped out of bed.

She had just washed and was beginning to dress when there was a knock on the door.

She guessed it would be Dawkins.

139

Quickly she put on her dressing-gown before she called out:

"Come in!"

Dawkins entered.

"'Is Lordship's compliments, Miss, an' will you put on your bonnet as you're goin' ashore immediately after breakfast."

"His Lordship is taking me with him?" Nikola asked excitedly.

"That's wot 'e said Miss," Dawkins replied. "A carriage is comin' to take you both to th' British Embassy."

He went out and shut the door.

Nikola stared at her reflection in the mirror, not seeing herself, but frightened by a new idea.

Perhaps the Marquis was handing her over to the British Ambassador.

His Excellency could send her back separately while he travelled alone in the Royal Carriages.

Nikola felt that once again the stone which had lain in her breast when she had been so frightened with Jimmy was back.

It was heavy and the sunshine had left the sky.

She put on the gown in which she had started the journey to Tilbury.

She was aware as she did so how shabby it looked.

She had nothing else, and anyway the Marquis would not notice.

"He has . . finished with . . me," she said in her heart.

She felt as if even *The Virgin in the Rose Garden* had deserted her.

She went up to find the Saloon empty except for a steward waiting with her breakfast.

"Where is His Lordship?" she could not help asking.

"'E's 'ad 'is breakfast, Miss an' 'e's givin' orders on th' Quay."

140

Quickly, because Nikola was afraid of keeping him waiting, she ate a few mouthfuls and drank a cup of coffee.

Then picked up her gloves, she went on deck.

On the Quay she saw there was a very impressive-looking carriage with the Royal Insignia on the doors.

For a moment she could not see the Marquis.

Then she saw him obviously giving instructions to the Second Mate and to Dawkins.

They were standing beside a Hackney carriage.

She walked down the gang-plank and he was waiting to assist her into the carriage from the British Embassy.

They drove off.

When they had gone quite a way in silence the Marquis suddenly said:

"I have something to ask you, Nikola."

She turned her head to look at him and he must have been aware she was nervous.

Also, because she was frightened, her lips trembled a little.

He looked at her for a long moment before he said:

"Do you love me, Nikola?"

It was such an utterly unexpected question that for a moment she could only stare at him.

Her eyes seemed to fill her whole face.

Because she was shy, the colour flooded into her cheeks.

Her eye-lashes flickered as she looked down.

The Marquis was waiting.

Until in a voice that seemed to come from a very long distance and was hardly audible, Nikola murmured:

"Y.yes."

"I thought I could not be mistaken," he said.

He looked away from her.

She thought miserably that now he had even taken away her pride.

141

Perhaps he felt sorry for her.

That would be even more agonising than loving him without his being aware of it.

They reached the gates of the British Embassy.

Nikola could see the Union Jack fluttered from the flagpole as the Marquis said:

"Do not be surprised at anything I may say in front of the Ambassador. Just agree with me."

She did not understand, but there was no time to ask questions.

The carriage came to a standstill.

An Aide-de-Camp was waiting for them in the open doorway.

As the sentries presented arms he greeted them respectfully.

Then he led them to a room where the Ambassador was waiting for them.

He was a good-looking man with greying hair and reminded her vaguely of her father.

"It is delightful to see you, My Lord," he said to the Marquis, "but I had no idea that you were in the vicinity until I learnt long after you had left that the Royal Carriages were at the station."

"I had reasons for going to Constantinople," the Marquis replied, "and now may I present Miss Tancombe, whom I discovered had no way of leaving that almost beleagured City."

The Ambassador shook Nikola by the hand saying:

"It must have been nerve-racking for you, Miss Tancombe."

Nikola smiled at him and the Marquis said:

"Now that I have brought her safely away, I should be married immediately!"

The Ambassador looked surprised while Nikola was frozen into immobility.

She felt she could not really have heard what the Marquis said.

Then as she stared at him, thinking she must have imagined it, he took her hand in his.

She felt his fingers squeeze hers and as he did so her heart turned a somersault.

She thought the whole room was so brilliant with sunshine that it hurt her eyes.

"Of course, My Lord, your marriage can be arranged," the Ambassador was saying. "I will send for my Chaplain."

"Thank you," the Marquis replied. "And now, as I have several things to discuss with you, perhaps my fiancée could rest in another room."

"I know my wife will be delighted to meet Miss Tancombe," the Ambassador replied.

He smiled at Nikola as he said:

"Let me take you to her."

Nikola looked at the Marquis.

He was smiling and there was an expression in his eyes that she could not interpret.

"Leave everything to me," he said so softly that only she could hear.

The Ambassador had reached the door and was opening it.

There was, therefore nothing Nikola could do but take one last look at the Marquis, then follow him.

They walked a little way to what she realised was the private part of the Embassy.

The Ambassadress was in a comfortable and attractive Sitting-Room.

The Ambassador introduced Nikola saying:

"This poor young lady has been incarcerated in Constantinople and only rescued by the Marquis of Ridgmont."

He smiled before he went on:

143

"He has asked that they should be married as soon as I can find my Chaplain. I am sure in the meantime, my dear, you will look after her."

"But of course!" the Ambassadress replied. "How exciting that you are to be married here! It must have been very frightening being in Constantinople with those awful Russians coming nearer and nearer every day!"

"It was . . wonderful to be with the Marquis," Nikola answered.

"And now you are to be married! It is very romantic!" the Ambassadress exclaimed.

Then as her eyes took in Nikola's appearance she said:

"I suppose, my dear, you have come away with very little luggage?"

"Very little," Nikola replied truthfully.

"I am sure we can do something about that," the Ambassadress remarked. "Now let me think – I have two daughters and one of them is, I am sure, about your size."

As she realised what she was going to say, Nikola clasped her hands together.

She knew she wanted above everything else to look beautiful for the Marquis.

Yet how was it possible to do so in a gown she had worn for four years and was, she was aware lamentably out of fashion?

"Come upstairs with me," the Ambassadress was saying.

Nikola was now even more certain than before that she was dreaming.

* * * * * * *

When the Ambassador returned to the Marquis, he said:

"My wife will look after Miss Tancombe, and let me, My Lord, congratulate you! She is certainly one of the most beautiful young women I have ever seen in my life!"

144

"That is what I think myself," the Marquis replied.

"And now tell me," the Ambassador went on, "What is happening in Constantinople?"

"I thought perhaps you had later news than I have," the Marquis replied. "We steamed here with all possible speed. When we left, the fate of Constantinople hung by a thread!"

The Ambassador smiled.

"Then I have good news for you," he said. "I heard only this morning that Admiral Thornby has been instructed to take his six battleships stationed in Besika Bay through the Dardanelles."

The Marquis sat back in his chair.

"That is exactly what I hoped would happen!" he exclaimed.

"It will certainly bring home to the Russians," the Ambassador said, "that Britain is to be considered in any further action taken by the Tsar, and will expect to be consulted about the terms of an Armistice."

"I hope you are right about that!" the Marquis said.

"If you ask me," the Ambassador went on, "and I have been very closely in touch with these things, the Grand Duke Nicolas is aware that the Russian Army is in no condition to fight a war with England."

The Marquis thought with satisfaction that his cable had woken up the Cabinet.

"I am told on good authority, and I am sure you will be able to confirm it," the Ambassador was saying, "that Russia has an empty treasury and an exhausted Army."

The Marquis did not reply and after a moment the Ambassador said quietly:

"I am not going to ask you, My Lord, what part you have played in this, as I am sure you will tell me to mind my own business. But we have every reason to celebrate the fact that Russia will not take Constantinople, and that you are to become a married man."

145

It was an hour later when Nikola came downstairs with the Ambassadress after having been told twice that the Chaplain was waiting for her.

"Let him wait," the Ambassadress said when the second summons arrived.

"Perhaps . . the Marquis . . will be . . angry," Nikola said a little nervously.

"He too can wait," the Ambassadress replied. "I know, my dear, he will think it worthwhile when he sees how lovely you look."

Her reflection in the mirror told Nikola that she was a very different person from the one she had seen on her arrival.

The Ambassadress had found her a white evening-gown belonging to her second daughter.

It fitted her so well that only one safety pin was necessary to tighten the waist a little.

A very lovely gown of soft chiffon, it had a bustle that flared out in a cascade of frills which ended in a little train on the ground.

The chiffon which draped Nikola's shoulders was sprinkled with tiny diamanté.

It made her look like a flower with dew-drops on the petals.

The Ambassadress's maid had arranged her hair in a fashionable manner.

As they had no wedding-veil they made one out of some yards of tulle which had been bought to trim a gown.

The softness of it made Nikola look ethereal.

The veil was held in place by a small tiara of diamonds which belonged to the Ambassadress.

"Now you really look like a Bride!" Her Excellency said with delight.

146

The maid opened the door and they walked slowly down the stairs.

An Aide-de-Camp gave her an admiring glance, then hurried to open the door into the Drawing-Room.

The Marquis and the Ambassador rose to their feet as Nikola entered.

She walked shyly towards them.

When she reached the Marquis he looked at her for a long moment before he said:

"That is exactly how I wanted you to look!"

"And that is what I wanted you to say!" the Ambassadress cried.

"The Chaplain is waiting," the Ambassador reminded them.

The Marquis walked to a chair at the side of the room.

Nikola saw that on it there was a bouquet of flowers which must have arrived when she was upstairs.

As the Marquis put it in her hands she saw that it was of roses.

She knew he had chosen it because of the picture of *The Virgin in the Rose Garden*.

She looked at him gratefully, and there was no need for words.

There was an expression in his eyes which she had never seen before.

It made her feel as if she reached up to touch the sky.

Then the Marquis offered his arm.

The Ambassador went ahead with his wife and they followed behind them towards the Chapel.

It was built out at the back of the Ambassy.

When they arrived the Chaplain was there in his surplice waiting to perform the Service.

Someone unseen was playing softly on the organ.

As the Marquis took Nikola up the aisle she felt her father and mother were near her and were aware of how happy she was.

The Chaplain read the beautiful words of the Marriage Service.

The Marquis placed on Nikola's finger his signet-ring.

To her it was the most valuable gift in the whole world.

With it he gave her a Heaven she had never dreamt she would enter.

They knelt for the blessing.

As they did so Nikola felt that it was her prayers to *The Virgin in the Rose Garden* that had brought them together.

Incredibly, unbelievably, the Marquis loved her!

As they left the Chapel she thought it would be an anticlimax to the beauty and sanctity of their marriage if they had to have luncheon in the Embassy.

To her joy, the Marquis took her to the front-door.

Outside she could see there was a carriage waiting.

"All our good wishes go with you both for your future happiness." the Ambassador said.

"I am very grateful to Your Excellency for everything," the Marquis replied.

The Ambassadress kissed Nikola.

"You are a very lucky girl, and the Marquis is a very lucky man," she said. "You will be one of the most beautiful Peeresses England has ever seen!"

"I only . . wish that was . . true," Nikola said.

"Send my tiara back with the carriage when you reach your yacht," the Ambassadress said, "but please keep the gown as a wedding-present."

"Do you really mean that?" Nikola asked.

"I ought to have given you a silver rose-bowl," the Ambassadress laughed, "but I feel this is more practical and my maid has also packed for you some day dresses, nightgowns and slippers."

"How can I thank you?" Nikola cried. "I am so very, very grateful."

She kissed the Ambassadress again before she got into the carriage.

The Marquis joined her and they drove away.

He took her hand in both of his and raised it to his lips.

"I do not . . believe . . this is . . true," Nikola murmured.

"It is true," the Marquis replied, "and I will tell you about it when we reach *The Sea Horse*."

The seamen had been busy while they were away.

The yacht was now decorated with flags and bunting.

Bunches of flowers were tied to the gang-plank.

They were piped aboard.

Then the crew, led by the Captain, gave them three hearty cheers.

The Marquis thanked them before he took Nikola into the Saloon.

It was then she remembered the Ambassadress's tiara.

The Marquis took it gently from her head and gave it to Dawkins.

He hurried back down the gang-plank to hand it to the coachman.

Then as Nikola took off her tulle veil, the yacht started to move.

Before they had left the harbour the steward had brought in their luncheon.

It was a light meal, but at the same time it was all the things Nikola liked best.

It was impossible however, to think of what she was eating.

She was only vividly and exclusively conscious of the Marquis sitting beside her.

He told her about the British Battleships steaming through the Dardanelles.

Although he did not say so, she knew he was responsible for them doing so.

"He is so . . clever and so . . wonderful," she told herself. "How can he . . love me?"

When they had finished luncheon and were alone, the Marquis said:

"I have a lot to talk to you about, my darling, and as I do not wish to be disturbed, I think we should go below."

If he had asked her to climb up a rainbow to Heaven, Nikola would have agreed.

She still could not believe that what had happened was real.

As they went down below she thought that at any moment she would wake up.

She would find herself alone in her cabin.

The Marquis did not take her into her cabin as she expected.

Instead he opened the door of his own.

She went in, then stood transfixed by what she saw.

The whole place was decorated with flowers.

Only as the scent of them fragrant on the air seemed to envelope her, did she realise they were all roses.

There were roses of almost every hue.

But the ones that encircled the back of the bed were white.

"How . . could . . you have thought of . . anything so lovely?" she exclaimed.

"How could I think of any other flower where you are concerned?" the Marquis asked. "I know, my precious, you have been praying to *The Virgin in the Rose Garden* ever since I have known you, and most especially when I was in danger."

"That is . . true," Nikola agreed, "but . . I thought that . . "

She looked away from him.

"You thought – what?" the Marquis asked.

" . . that you were . . bored with me," she whispered.

"Bored?" he exclaimed. "It has been an indescribable torture not to hold you close to me and kiss you after we had left Constantinople."

150

"Then . . why?" she asked, "why . . were you so . . distant? I . . I do not . . understand."

The Marquis put his arms around her and they sat down on the side of the bed.

"My precious," he said, "when I kissed you because I knew the Russians were listening outside, I knew that I loved you as I have never loved a woman before."

He pulled her a little closer.

His lips moved over the softness of her cheek before he went on:

"I knew, too, that you felt the same rapture that I did, and that we were meant for each other since the beginning of time."

"Why . . why did . . you not . . tell me so?" Nikola whispered.

"Because, my precious, I brought you on this journey for my own convenience, as a companion."

He paused to smile at her before he continued:

"I never imagined for one moment that I would fall in love with you. When I did, I knew you were everything I wanted in my wife."

Nikola made a little murmur and hid her face against his neck.

"As my wife," the Marquis went on, "I wanted you exactly as you were – pure, holy and untouched until I could put a ring on your finger and know that you were mine."

"H.how could I have . . guessed what you were . . feeling?" Nikola murmured.

"What I was feeling was a wild and violent desire to kiss you and to awaken you to the wonder of love. But I knew you would think it wrong until we were actually married."

Now Nikola understood.

She thought no man could have been more sensitive or more intuitive of what she might have felt had he done so.

151

"Now you are mine," the Marquis said in his deep voice, "and this, my precious, is what I have been waiting for. I shall no longer have to lie awake at night because I need you."

He paused a moment and then went on:

"I did not dare to look at you in case I kissed you as I wanted to until I could no longer think, but only feel."

"I . . love you! I . . love . . you . . .!" Nikola breathed.

She knew they were the words that had made her cry every night.

She had thought she would never be able to say them aloud.

"As I love you!" the Marquis said.

She had looked up at him as she spoke and now his lips came down on hers.

He kissed her at first gently, as if she was infinitely precious.

Somehow the sanctity of their marriage was still with them.

Then there were little flames of ecstasy throbbing within him.

He knew Nikola was feeling the same, and his lips became more possessive.

She felt that she melted into him.

She was so bemused by the wonder of what he aroused in her that she was hardly aware when he drew her to her feet.

Gently he undid the back of the chiffon gown she had worn for her wedding.

He lifted her onto the rose-encircled bed.

Only as he did so did she realise that she was naked.

Shyly she pulled the sheet over her breasts.

Then the roses seemed to come nearer.

The scent of them intensified and the Marquis was beside her.

He drew her into his arms.

152

She felt his heart beating as violently as it had when the Russians had threatened him.

But now it was beating with love, not with fear.

She looked up at him and he thought it was impossible for anyone to look more beautiful.

"Am I . . really your . . wife?"

"That is what I am going to prove to you, my lovely darling," he answered, "but I am afraid of frightening you, as you were when I first saw you."

"I was . . frightened then because Jimmy and I had . . done something . . wrong," Nikola answered, "but . . this is right! I know we have been . . joined together by God . . and of course . . by *The Virgin in the Rose Garden* who protected you from the Russians."

"She brought you to me," the Marquis said, "and when we hang the picture in our bedroom at Ridge, we can look at it together and realise how blessed we are."

Nikola gave a little cry and put her arms around his neck.

"You understand? Oh, my wonderful . . magnificent husband . . you understand!"

"What I understand is that I have been looking for you, although I was not aware of it, all my life," he answered. "Now that I have found you, I will never let you go. You are mine, Nikola, mine completely and absolutely and I will love and worship you unto eternity!"

Then he was kissing her.

Kissing her wildly, demandingly passionately.

She felt her love become a flame which quickened and joined the flame within him.

It carried them high into the sky.

They were part of the sun, the moon, the stars, and also the roses which came from God.

. . . .

It was very much later.

The sun had lost its strength and soon darkness would cover the world.

"I . . love . . you!" Nikola murmured.

She had said it a hundred times before, although the words always seemed to be new.

"You are perfect!" the Marquis said.

He knew it was perfection he had never expected to find in any woman.

He added with a little smile:

"I have one present for you, but you will have to wait until we reach Paris for the rest."

"We are . . going to . . Pa:is?" Nikola asked.

"To buy you a trousseau, my precious, and it will be very exciting to dress you so that you look even more beautiful than you are at this moment!"

Then he laughed and said:

"Actually I prefer you with nothing!"

Nikola blushed.

"You are . . making me . . feel shy," she said accusingly.

"I adore you when you are shy," the Marquis said.

He pulled her closer to him.

Then as if he must finish what he was saying he said:

"Now you have some pretty clothes to wear we will stop in Venice."

"Oh, I would . . love . . that!" Nikola exclaimed.

"The Royal Carriages will meet us there and this time there will be no lobby between you and me."

"We will . . be . . together in the . . Queen's bed," Nikola murmured.

"As long as I can make love to you, it does not matter where we are," the Marquis replied.

His hand was on her breast but he remembered what he had promised her.

"Let me give you your first present."

He bent down and picked up something off the floor.

Without Nikola realising it, he had brought a newspaper from the Saloon.

It was "The Morning Post," a week old.

The Marquis had folded the pages.

As he handed it to Nikola there was one piece of news in the centre which he obviously wanted her to read.

She took it from him, wondering what it was that could concern her.

Then she read:

"TRAGEDY OF A DISTINGUISHED PEERESS

Lady Hartley, the widow of Lord Hartley of Melcombe, was killed in a tragic accident which happened near her home in Essex.

Driving in her carriage drawn by two horses the shaft broke and injured one horse, sending him wild. The two animals galloped down a steep hill with the coachman unable to stop them, and crashing into a narrow bridge at the bottom of it, turned the carriage over. The coachman escaped with a few injuries and slight concussion.

Lady Hartley was however crushed by the vehicle and died a few hours later after she had been taken to a neighbouring house.

Before she died, however, Lady Hartley made a new Will. She left her white cat Snowball, her house and all her possessions to her nephew Sir James Tancombe 10th Baronet of King's Keep, Hertfordshire.

Sir James is at present abroad and the Solicitors are making every endeavour to get in touch with him."

Nikola read the story to its end, then gave an audible gasp.

The Marquis was watching her.

Then suddenly she laughed.

155

"*Snowball!* It was Jimmy who gave Aunt Alice *Snowball* and that is why she has left him everything she possessed!"

She laughed again.

"You do see, my wonderful husband," she went on, "that after all, Jimmy has not stolen *The Virgin in the Rose Garden* because it is now his!"

"That is something I shall contest very forcefully!" the Marquis replied. "It is ours, my darling, and we will never allow anyone to take it away from us."

"Yes . . it is ours," Nikola agreed.

She threw the newspaper down beside the bed and lifted her face to her husband's.

Other books by Barbara Cartland

Romantic Novels, over 400, the most recently published being:

Love is a Maze
A Circus for Love
The Temple of Love
The Bargain Bride
The Haunted Heart
Real Love or Fake
A Kiss from a Stranger
A Very Special Love
A Necklace of Love
A Revolution of Love

The Marquis Wins
Love is the Key
Free as the Wind
Desire in the Desert
A Heart in the Highlands
The Music of Love
The Wrong Duchess
The Taming of a Tigress
Love Comes to the Castle
The Magic of Paris

The Dream and the Glory (In aid of the St. John Ambulance Brigade)

Autobiographical and Biographical:

The Isthmus Years 1919–1939
The Years of Opportunity 1939–1945
I Search for Rainbows 1945–1976
We Danced All Night 1919–1929
Ronald Cartland (With a foreword by Sir Winston Churchill)
Polly – My Wonderful Mother
I Seek the Miraculous

Historical:

Bewitching Women
The Outrageous Queen (The Story of Queen Christina of Sweden)
The Scandalous Life of King Carol
The Private Life of Charles II
The Private Life of Elizabeth, Empress of Austria
Josephine, Empress of France
Diane de Poitiers
Metternich – The Passionate Diplomat
A Year of Royal Days
Royal Lovers
Royal Jewels
Royal Eccentrics

Sociology:

You in the Home
The Fascinating Forties
Marriage for Moderns
Be Vivid, Be Vital
Love, Life and Sex
Vitamins for Vitality
Husbands and Wives
Men are Wonderful
Etiquette
The Many Facets of Love
Sex and the Teenager
The Book of Charm
Living Together
The Youth Secret
The Magic of Honey
The Book of Beauty and Health
Keep Young and Beautiful by Barbara Cartland and Elinor Glyn
Etiquette for Love and Romance
Barbara Cartland's Book of Health

General:

Barbara Cartland's Book of Useless Information with a Foreword by the
    Earl Mountbatten of Burma.
  (In aid of the United World Colleges)
Love and Lovers (Picture Book)
The Light of Love (Prayer Book)
Barbara Cartland's Scrapbook
(In aid of the Royal Photographic Museum)
Romantic Royal Marriages
Barbara Cartland's Book of Celebrities
Getting Older, Growing Younger

Verse:

Lines on Life and Love

Music:

An Album of Love Songs
sung with the Royal Philharmonic Orchestra.

Films:

A Hazard of Hearts
The Lady and the Highwayman
A Ghost in Monte Carlo
Duel of Love

Cartoons:

Barbara Cartland Romances (Book of Cartoons)
has recently been published in the U.S.A., Great Britain,
and other parts of the world.

Children:

A Children's Pop-Up Book: "Princess to the Rescue"

Cookery:

Barbara Cartland's Health Food Cookery Book
Food for Love
Magic of Honey Cookbook
Recipes for Lovers
The Romance of Food

Editor of:

"The Common Problem" by Ronald Cartland (with a preface by the Rt.
  Hon. the Earl of Selborne, P.C.)
Barbara Cartland's Library of Love
        Library of Ancient Wisdom
"Written with Love" Passionate love letters selected by Barbara
  Cartland

Drama:

Blood Money
French Dressing

Philosophy:

Touch the Stars

Radio Operetta:

The Rose and the Violet
(Music by Mark Lubbock) Performed in 1942.

Radio Plays:

The Caged Bird: An episode in the life of Elizabeth Empress of Austria.
  Performed in 1957.